FACING THE BRIDGE

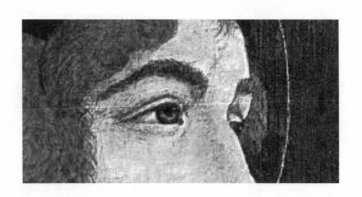

FACING THE BRIDGE

Yoko Tawada

translated and with an Afterword by
MARGARET MITSUTANI

A NEW DIRECTIONS PAPERBOOK ORIGINAL

"The Shadow Man" was originally published as "Kage otoko" in the book *Futakuchi-
otoko* (Kawade-shobo-shinsa, 1998); "In Front of Trang Tien Bridge" was originally
published as "Chantien bashi no mae nite" in the book *Hikari to Zelachin no Leipzig*
(Kodansha, 2000); "Saint George and the Translator" was originally published as
"Arufabetto no kizuguchi" in the book *Arufabetto no kizuguchi* (Kawade-shobo-shinsa,
1993).

Manufactured in the United States of America
New Directions Books are printed on acid-free paper
First published as a New Directions Paperbook Original (NDP1070) in 2007
Published simultaneously in Canada by Penguin Books Canada Limited

Library of Congress Cataloging-in-Publication Data

Tawada, Yoko, 1960-
  Facing the bridge / Yoko Tawada ; translated from the Japanese by Margaret
Mitsutani.
    p. cm.
  ISBN-13: 978-0-8112-1690-6 (alk. paper)
  ISBN-10: 0-8112-1690-X (alk. paper)
I. Tawada, Yoko, 1960—Translations into English. II. Mitsutani, Margaret,
  1953- III. Title.
PL862.A85A6 2007
895.6'35—dc22   2007001148

New Directions Books are published for James Laughlin
by New Directions Publishing Corporation
80 Eighth Avenue, New York, NY 10011

Contents

The Shadow Man

1

The world was turning upside down and the elders didn't speak, their hips moving sluggishly. Amo watched them, burning with frustration. This was his first memory. In the bay they called "The Goddess's Chamber" where the jungle ended and the sea began, there should have been only gentle waves moving drowsily in and out, but during the night what looked like a huge temple had appeared and in the morning Bad Spirits descended from it, one after another. With boxes wrapped in scarlet cloth clutched to their chests, the Bad Spirits rowed to shore in a stream of small boats. The elders stared blankly, not even touching their weapons. And when the Bad Spirits solemnly offered their gifts the elders snatched them away, their eager fingers fumbling with the cloth. Amo couldn't imagine what made their lips take on such a honeyed look, mouths half open in ecstasy. They irritated him. Were they all drunk on the maya-maya fruit? Whenever they ate it their eyes rolled back in their heads and they drooled, no longer hearing what you said. Limp as lizards' tails, kicked or screamed at, they wouldn't get angry. Had they been gobbling that fruit again? Amo hid in the thorny bushes, standing perfectly still. His uncle disappeared into the jungle with the others but once their treasure was safely hidden, they all returned to the beach. Offering a second round of presents, the Bad Spirits pointed again and again toward the temple. Then they formed pairs and, grabbing his uncle and the others by the arms, one on each side, they shoved them into the small boats and rowed out to it. No one resisted. They didn't even raise their voices. Amo wasn't afraid of the floating temple or the Bad Spirits, but it horrified him to see the elders so passive. These men with nerves attuned to the slightest rustling in the grass, who could react as swiftly as a dart from a blowpipe, who could run like whirligig beetles darting across the water when danger was near, now meekly obeyed the Bad Spirits without fighting back. The Spirits wrapped their feet in leather bags, covered their legs, stomachs, chests and arms with cloth, and dyed their hair reddish-brown. Their eyes melted in the sunlight and looked almost white.

Amo heard footsteps behind him. He turned around and saw one of the Bad Spirits standing there, and when their eyes met the Spirit knelt to the ground and held out both hands, which were filled with gleaming white powder. Since no elder had ever shown him such deference Amo was startled at first, but then a warm feeling came over him and he let the Spirit spill some of the pristine powder into his own palms. When he licked the powder, it tasted so sweet a pain darted through his chin. Was the Spirit young or old? It had the bright, round eyes of a kangaroo rat, and wrinkles on its forehead as deep as his grandfather's. From its smell Amo knew it must be very, very old, but then why was there so much fat on its stomach? Didn't only children's bellies protrude like that? His memory of what happened next wasn't clear. The tickling sensation of feathers on his chest and belly; the blood-colored drink that felt so cool going down before sending him into a dreamy haze; food that made his mouth water just to look at it. Arms around his shoulders; pats on the head; light, encouraging slaps on the back. He told himself over and over that this was all a dream. If he wasn't dreaming he'd have to find his family at once and help them escape. But if he was dreaming, he could stay in this half-sleep until he woke up. Amo was taken to a ship's cabin—table, sofa, patterned plants drawn on the walls. Next door was a bedroom where he slept at night, pressed against a big man like a baby animal huddled against its mother. Unlike the muscular bodies of his father and the other elders, this man's belly consisted of a soft layer of fat, and was as white as a fish's with coarse, golden hair growing out of it. The Spirits called him Heer, so Amo did likewise. Were his brothers and sisters sleeping in such a way, too, in different rooms on the ship? Whenever the possibility occurred to him he suddenly became frightened and stopped thinking. Among his fourteen siblings Amo had two older brothers he was especially close to, and now, remembering how they'd always been together, his skin longed for their touch. Overcome with yearning for them one night, he slipped out of the cabin. As he walked through the dim corridors that laced the ship like blood vessels, the stench of rotting animal flesh stung his nostrils through the harsh, salty sea air. Above the drone of the ship, he heard the murmurs and groans of curses. He recalled a warning not to go down to the sea alone at night. A dark shadow appeared out of nowhere; Amo was punched in the nose and fainted. The next morning when he woke up, Heer was bathing his forehead with a wet cloth. A terrible odor, unlike any Amo had smelled before, seemed to be rising from his own pores. Heer told him how dangerous it was to leave the cabin alone. "Because I've chosen you, as long as you're here with me no harm can come to you; but the people out there are different and may treat you badly, so you must never go walking around by yourself." Heer often sounded like a fortune-teller. Without actually studying the language, Amo was able to understand everything Heer said to him by the time he stepped off the boat.

When they arrived in Amsterdam, the sailors cheered and cheered with tears in their eyes. To Amo, it seemed a

YOKO TAWADA

desolate land. There was no sound, and the few trees standing here and there had no leaves. The sun was wrapped in smoke; the smell of smoked fish rose among the rows of stone houses. The people looked cold, wrapped in layer upon layer of clothes. They hardly decorated themselves at all, especially the men.

Amo received the name Anton Wilhelm from the minister. Heer, he was told, would be his father from now on. In Heer's house, both men and women slept under the same roof. In the village where Amo was born, from the age of five girls lived in the women's house and boys in the men's. Here he was returned to the care of females who dressed him up in various kinds of clothing, took him by the hand, and stood him in front of a mirror several times a day. In the mirror, their hands fluttered like butterflies. They touched him everywhere, reminding him of when he was still a baby, always being handled by women. Now that he was seven, their palms felt unpleasantly warm and sticky. But if Heer deemed this proper he would have to put up with them no matter how strange it felt. Heer was often away for meetings, business deals, planning sessions, and banquets. Except for an old servant, Amo rarely saw men. These females constantly stroked Amo, marveling at the ebony smoothness of his chest. They pinched his buttocks on the sly. The maid whose big, yellow teeth showed when she laughed would grab his penis when no one was looking and not let go. Amo stared at the boy in the mirror as if he were looking at a ghost. Why did he look so different? Everyone else had pale faces and skin with open pores and golden brown hair. Amo's skin was black and shiny, with no hair anywhere except on his head.

The women fed Amo meat and potatoes from silver platters. At night, they put him to bed and sang him lullabies. As he watched the child in the mirror grow prettier each day, Amo thought that no matter where they decided to take him he wouldn't mind as long as he could be with this beautiful boy.

Tamao found himself once again standing before a shop window examining the reflection of a young Japanese man. Since arriving in Wolfenbüttel, he'd never once been attracted by the goods on display behind the glass. Huddled in a gray-brown interior, they had nothing to say to him. Like all foreign students, Tamao didn't have much money, so if there was nothing he wanted to buy all the better. Then why was he so obsessed with his reflection in the glass? His chest and hips seemed somehow deficient, and the delicate line from his shoulders to his fingertips looked positively effeminate. He never studied himself this way before, as if he were a stranger from some faraway place. Occasionally, he used to glance in a mirror to check out his new glasses or to see if the cut on his chin had healed, but in such instances he was only examining a certain part of his face. Here in Wolfenbüttel he found himself searching for full-length mirrors that would give him the whole picture.

"Here to see the sights?" The man who suddenly appeared beside him was shaped like a barrel, with a bushy beard that looked like a lion's mane. Tamao hurriedly turned away from the window.

"I am here to study philosophy." Casting a sidelong glance, Tamao replied as if reading from a textbook. The fellow's thin lips tightened in a scornful laugh. "One of Amo's descendents."

Tamao had never heard of Amo, but afraid of being chided for his ignorance, he decided not to ask about him.

"Did some philosophy myself a while back, but got fed up and quit," the man said, searching Tamao's face for an answer he was determined not to miss.

"Are you sure it wasn't philosophy that got sick of you?" Tamao shot back with just the right measure of sarcasm. He was feeling pleased with himself until the man's lips stiffened into the shape of a dragonfly and began to twitch. Startled, Tamao blurted out, "Sorry, got to go now," and started to walk away, but it was already too late.

"What made you take up philosophy anyway?" the fellow roared, ready for a fight. While Tamao fumbled for an answer the man let out a piercing laugh and announced that his name was Manfred, not that anyone had asked. So this is how one makes acquaintances here, Tamao thought, feeling as if he were watching a poorly written television drama. Beads of sweat the size of rice grains appeared on

Manfred's forehead. His lips formed the vowels like an actor practicing voice projection, but no sound emerged. He didn't even seem aware that his mouth was moving. There's something strange about this guy, thought Tamao.

2

Purely by accident, Amo learned that he was to be given away as a present. While walking back and forth in the great hall as he always did, stopping to gaze at the picture on a Chinese vase or peer into the darkness of the unused fireplace, he heard someone being shown into the parlor next door. After greeting Heer, the visitor quickly stated his business. Amo didn't understand what they were talking about, nor did it interest him, but his ears pricked up at the mention of his name. Heer sounded reluctant, replying in monosyllables, while his guest spoke ever more enthusiastically about Amo. As he listened to this total stranger speak his name as if this were perfectly natural, Amo grew frightened. Hadn't his uncle warned him never to tell a stranger his name? Once people know your name, they can change your whole life, his uncle told him. Then Amo overheard the word "present." He thought of that boy in the mirror, so beautifully dressed. Wrapped in bright, shiny paper and tied with ribbons, like a gift. When the women were han-

YOKO TAWADA

dling him, they squealed with delight. Could that boy be a present? When the visitor left, Heer called Amo into his study. "You'll be leaving Amsterdam soon, and going to a place called Wolfenbüttel; when you arrive, you must think of the Duke of Braunschweig as your father and serve him well." Upon learning there would be a dog in his new home, Amo was overjoyed and pranced around the room. An acquaintance of Heer's kept two dogs in his house, and Amo wanted one so badly he didn't know what to do. He wasn't quite ten years old the day he moved to Wolfenbüttel.

Traveling didn't upset Amo in the least. Wherever he went, grownup men dressed in fine clothes were there to meet him. He had only to ask, and they would give him whatever he wanted. He readily accepted the notion of a "father" as an interchangeable guardian. When they heard Amo was leaving, all the women in Heer's house, from maid to cook to gardener's daughter, wept aloud. They annoyed Amo with their sticky tears and high-pitched, ear-splitting wails. Glad to get away, he scrambled into the carriage and let out a cheer. As they rolled along, he bounced his bottom up and down to the rhythm of the wheels. The scenery flew by, each image dissolving in an instant so that looking back he could only see gritty dust. Amo asked his traveling companion, a youth of about twenty, if he, too, was a gift for someone in Wolfenbüttel, but the young man said he was going to become a scholar. When he saw Amo's eyes widen with curiosity, the youth explained that a scholar was someone who read and wrote books. The way he pronounced the word "book" sounded so delicious that Amo immediately began to yearn for one.

The Duke of Braunschweig's face was flat and pale. The folds in his overflowing clothes were far more expressive, reminding Amo of vines in the jungle. When Amo recited the greeting he had learned in the carriage, only the Duke's eyes moved in response.

Amo soon learned German. Any word he heard once was embedded in his memory like a design carved into a clay pot. He could listen to a sentence and repeat it aloud the following day, even if he didn't understand what the words meant. When he uncomprehendingly recited an expression he fancied, his listeners would burst out laughing or their eyes would widen in surprise. Their reactions delighted him. The women here were different from the ones in Amsterdam. They weren't so interested in touching his skin, and they never laughed in creaky voices like an old door that needed oiling. The maids assigned to the parts of the house where Amo lived—the bedroom, the great hall, and the dining room—were quietly efficient, their faces as grim as hunters armed with bows and arrows. There was only one middle-aged lady, a distant relative of the Duke's, whose dry lips stretched into a wide smile whenever she saw him, and who spoke softly to him, placing a hand gently on his shoulder as if he were very fragile. Without what was called a husband, she was kept quietly inside the Duke's mansion with no special role to play or tasks to perform. The old cook addressed her as Fräulein, so Amo thought he'd try calling her that, too. The woman breathed out gusts of silent laughter, and held him tightly to her breast. To everyone here he was Anton. But a name other people used was merely something given from the outside—it had nothing to do with your real self. Amo felt sure he once had a true name, although try as he might he couldn't remember it. Fräulein showed him an illustrated volume of Bible stories from which she would read to him, occasionally making up stories of her own. Since coming here he looked not at mirrors but at books. Listening to Fräulein's stories as he gazed at the pictures, Amo felt his body would surely be absorbed into that separate world. The people in the illustrations draped themselves with gold or red cloth, leaving only their hands and faces uncovered. Diamond-shaped eyes shone with a raw brilliance. The world in books sometimes reminded him of the jungle, too. Every page began with a huge illuminated letter, broad enough to be a patch of grassland surrounded by a fence. Each letter-enclosure contained a tangle of vines with birds and dogs and humans playing together. Some of the animals' hind legs were ensnared by the vines, turning the animals into plants from the waist down. It seemed a hundred years to Amo since he walked through the jungle. There you must be alert to many signs. Animal tracks, for instance, or thorny and poisonous plants, snakes or scorpions, the various cries of birds, smells in the air. When reading you simply move on to the next word, but in the jungle you need to look everywhere, especially behind you. There is no need to worry about what you've already read. You stay focused on what is ahead, and keep your eyes moving forward. Learning letters didn't take much effort for Amo. Before long he could easily find his way through any book without Fräulein's help. As he read he felt he was chanting a magic spell that would keep the Bad Spirits away. Was it really Bad Spirits who had risen out of the ocean and taken his uncle and other family away? Where could they have gone? Could the world he had once known have completely disappeared? At times he wanted to ask Fräulein about that voyage across the sea, but whenever he tried, his throat hurt and he lost his voice. If those were Bad Spirits who had appeared in the bay, then perhaps everyone here, including Fräulein, was in league with them. As long as Amo pretended to forget what happened that day, everyone would be kind to him. But wasn't this only because they mistakenly believed him to be one of them? If so, he would continue to let them dwell in their misunder-standing. Whenever a violent storm arose, his uncle and the other grownups would calm the fury of the Bad Spirits by putting on masks to show that they were Bad Spirits, too; surely this was what Amo was doing now. As long as he pre-tended to be one of them, they would do him no harm. The moment he started screaming for his father, his uncle, his cousins, his brothers and sisters, the eyes in those kind faces would instantly turn red, the canine teeth would grow into fangs, and with hooked claws that had once been fingernails the Bad Spirits would grab Amo by his kinky hair and drown him in a swamp.

One day Amo was sitting with Fräulein in the great hall looking at a map of the world when the Duke of Braunschweig entered. Fräulein handed Amo a book with a knowing look, and he proceeded to smoothly read out the Latin text for her as he always did. The Duke of Braunschweig's gloomy countenance lit up as he let out an "Oh!" of surprise. Suddenly nervous, Amo stole a glance at the Duke's face. His narrowed eyes were shining like a fish's belly. Fräulein stood at his side, beaming with pride in her victory.

Beginning the following week a series of men visited Amo in turn to teach him foreign languages, dead languages, history, medicine, astrology, and other subjects. Like an old tool that has outlived its usefulness, Fräulein was relegated to a back room. Amo was always cheerful on days when his tutors came; he started to grow very quickly. Fräulein eventually contracted a lung disease, and took to her bed in one of the outbuildings. Amo went to see her every day at first, but as the weeks passed his visits became less and less frequent until he finally forgot all about her.

Tamao came to study here, where Lessing once lived, through the introduction of Professor Kanatsu. The town offered a one-year scholarship to students from his university who were studying the German playwright, and Professor Meyer, an old friend of Professor Kanatsu's who had retired several years earlier, recommended Tamao. This elderly German professor, whom he had not met before, phoned to invite him to dinner. Tamao anxiously wondered about what he should wear, and what he should say. A suit seemed like the safest bet, though while examining himself in the mirror wearing a coat and tie, all he could see was a used car salesman. And what if he blurted out some foolish remark that made the Professor regret his recommendation? Keeping his mouth shut wasn't an option, either. He had learned from a friend who had studied here that Germans considered silence a sign of stupidity. So if the Professor wanted to know what he thought of Germany, Tamao would say he found the tranquil atmosphere ideal for the scholarly life. If asked about the food, he would tell him how impressive he found the long tradition of bread making. What he really dreaded were inquiries into the exact nature of his research on Lessing. To tell the truth, he was studying Lessing because Professor Kanatsu had told him to. Not that he wasn't interested, or didn't have a fundamental grasp of Lessing's work; he simply wasn't prepared to give a scholarly explanation of what he intended to focus on or why. However, he couldn't very well reveal that he didn't know what he wanted to do. Tamao's mind was in such turmoil he could hardly see the door in front of him, so when it opened, he missed the chance to thrust out his hand for the Professor to shake. A gentle smile on his face, his eyes surrounded by tiny wrinkles, the Professor looked rather like an old woman. As men age, something feminine seems to take up residence in their faces. The Professor's wife, made up like a Barbie doll, seemed much younger. Surrounded by art deco furniture and Chinese porcelain from the Han period that might have been fake but looked impressive anyway, Tamao became terribly nervous. A glass of white wine was placed in his hand as he stood there talking with the Professor.

"Is Professor Kanatsu well? It's been more than fifteen years since I've been in Tokyo—the city must have changed."

More harmless questions were beginning to relax him until a huge German shepherd padded out from one of the inner rooms. Tamao, who hated dogs, clutched his wineglass in both hands and struggled to keep from quivering all over. The beast sniffed at his shoes. Immediately sensing Tamao's terror, Professor Meyer laughed heartily and said, "Our guest doesn't like dogs, so you run along now." Without further ado, the shepherd turned around and left the room. At dinner, the pork and potatoes and green beans Tamao took from the silver platter in the center of the table rolled around on his plate like sunbathers on a beach. Tamao was not a big eater, and meat never agreed with him, but remembering his friend saying that with enough practice anyone could eat loads of meat, he attacked the slab like a warrior facing battle. He was so engrossed in his fight with the pork that when Professor Meyer suddenly inquired, "Do you have any brothers and sisters?" he wasn't sure for a moment whether he did or not. He broke into a cold sweat. Could he have forgotten that he had a brother after only a week in Germany? But if he were to answer, "I have an older brother," the question "What does he do?" would naturally follow. He would be embarrassed to admit that his brother was doing nothing but dinky part-time jobs. The Professor and his wife surely wouldn't approve. What kind of future would they see for the younger brother of someone like that? Tamao finally decided to reply, "No, I'm an only child."

The meat, which had looked lean enough, turned into a chunk of solid grease on its way down his throat. After a while, the Professor said, "Many Japanese come here to study music. Do you like music?" At Tamao's answer, "Yes, I love Wagner. I have his complete works," the Professor's face darkened. Realizing he'd said something he shouldn't have, he quickly added, "But I like Michael Jackson, too," in what he meant to be an engaging manner, but this time, the Professor's wife grimaced.

When he watched Michael Jackson's videos, every cell in Tamao's body started to seethe; he even felt his appearance begin to change. His friends all said plastic surgery was in bad taste. But didn't everyone harbor a secret desire for a new face? His own was as plain as a burlap sack, so he put it out of his mind and studied hard to compensate for how dull he looked. He told himself that fretting over one's appearance was a job for women. But deep down, doesn't every man who lacks confidence in his looks yearn for that moment when the Beast turns into a handsome young man?

As he watched Tamao take a second helping of green beans and the smallest piece of meat, the Professor quickly remarked, "You like vegetables, don't you? That's good for your health," and laughed. The Professor certainly was observant. In a town this size, where you could go anywhere on foot, it would be impossible to keep anything, no matter how small, a secret. Nothing ever really happened here, so outsiders were carefully watched, examined, assessed. If you rated highly enough, they would probably accept you. In a big city you would forever remain a stranger without a name, so perhaps it was actually easier for foreign elements to be welcomed into a little place like this, Tamao concluded.

3

On the days his tutors came, Amo felt bright and sunny inside. Of course each tutor was of a different type: some sat in front of him like a wall spouting knowledge, while others treated him like a friend. Herr Kaiser, the Latin teacher, acted like Amo didn't exist, droning on and on as if reading to himself, occasionally glancing down at his pupil as if he were a piece of broken pottery. Herr Kaiser also never laughed. Even so, Amo found Latin grammar as much fun as a puzzle. Herr Petersen, who taught history and literature, was just the opposite, bending over to look him in the eye as though they were planning some mischief together, chatting confidentially through the lesson. Poring over a map seemed to give Herr Petersen the illusion that he was aboard a ship, for he would gaze up at the dark ceiling as if it were a blinding sun, and sway back and forth as he talked, tossed by imaginary waves.

At the mention of ships, Amo's whole body stiffened. He had nightmares about them. When he awoke with a cry the boat would be gone, and much to his relief, he'd find that the legs of his bed were planted firmly on the floor. Sometimes he had similar dreams during the day, when he dozed off on the sofa after lunch. The lurid colors he saw in these daytime nightmares made them even more terrifying than the ones he had at night. The ship in his dreams always possessed a complex web of corridors; Amo would be feeling his way down a dark, narrow staircase, or crouching to squeeze through a tiny entrance, crawling further and further into the interior of a snail. He didn't know what he was searching for. But then a door covered with black mold would appear, and though he dreaded opening it, someone would push him from behind, sending him sprawling straight into it. The door would crumble softly like a wall kneaded from wet earth, and Amo would pop out on the other side. His nose would hit the floor; then, planting his hands on the damp stickiness, he would lift himself up. The place reeked of blood and rotting flesh. Knowing this stench might draw hyenas, he would anxiously look around. As his eyes adjusted to the darkness he'd see prostrate human figures. What he had mistaken for the rumble of the sea was actually the moaning of men. Rows and rows of men. Amo would peer cautiously into their faces: drawn, swollen, with sunken cheeks. The flesh of some men would be torn from their shoulders like rags, revealing white bone underneath. Something would be crawling among the bones, a mass of movement.

Amo was always relieved when dawn finally came after a sleepless night. The maid would bring cold water in a china basin. As he stood in the water while she washed his sweaty skin, the oppression of the nightmare would gradually lift, and his chest would lighten. By the time his tutor appeared and the books were open, the dream would be far away.

Sometimes Herr Petersen asked Amo how he'd slept the night before. Even when he didn't feel tired, his eyelids drooped a little, giving him a sleepy look. He never told Herr Petersen about his nightmares. If this kindly tutor were to know about his ship dream, Amo was certain the connection between them would be severed.

He had another recurring nightmare about sharks. As he

gazed at the sea the wind skimmed its surface, creating a lovely pattern of waves that opened out before his eyes. Something, though, was not quite right. Why didn't the water flow naturally, and what was that nasty glare? he wondered. Then it was too late. Amo would be gulping seawater as the waves pulled him under and, before he knew what was happening, he'd be sucked straight into a shark's mouth. Teeth sprouted like icicles above and below; through them he could see water and sky. Perhaps he could jump out if he set his mind to it. But his uncle had told him that a shark has three rows of teeth. Even if you managed to get past the first, the second would surely crush your backbone. And if you succeeded in maneuvering through the second, then the third would come crashing down on you. He simply couldn't muster the courage to jump. It was definitely much safer to stay here, inside. Through the window of the shark's mouth, he could see the ship. On board, the Bad Spirits were hurling people into the sea. Perhaps the people had already lost consciousness, for they didn't cry out or struggle, but fell in like dead weight. Other sharks rose to the surface, their fins breaking the water, gleaming like metal as black blood stained the seafoam.

A magnificent cherry tree with spreading branches stands in front of Lessing's house. Tamao was secretly proud of it. People thought of this as the symbol of *Japan*—not bad, he thought. Every time he went out, he made a point of walking by the tree. Even if he had to go

YOKO TAWADA

out of his way, it wasn't far in such a small town. Today, though, he saw a Japanese woman walking toward him from beyond the tree. Tamao was shocked. His first thought was, I mustn't let her take my tree away. The figure grew larger. Tamao wanted to erase her from the scene.

"Well, hello. Are you from Japan, too?" the woman asked. Her greeting was a bit loud, though not too annoying. The next bit was what really grated on him. Her name was Nana, and she was also a student, paying her own way. As she didn't have much money saved, she was working part-time at a Chinese restaurant. Lessing was her specialty, and she was now working on her M.A. thesis. Tamao seethed inside, and nearly blurted out, What makes you think you understand Lessing? The very idea of there being *two* Japanese people in such little town at the same time, both with the same research topic, seemed unbearable to him.

"No use studying Lessing in this day and age," Tamao countered, digging earnestly at the ground with his right shoe. He felt a sneer spread from his mouth up to his nose.

"Why do you say that?" Nana looked straight at him, not even bothering to brush back her hair blowing across her face, which irritated Tamao even more. He began to ask her what meaning 18th-century Enlightenment could possibly have today, now that even postmodernism was over and done with, but Nana cut him off with a torrent of words. She talked on and on as if censuring someone who wasn't there, speaking so fast he hardly had time to digest what she was saying. "Even if the three great religions make peace by signing some sort of civil contract, it would be like three sons killing their younger sisters and then sitting down to discuss their inheritance rights," she said, and finally realizing that she was talking about Lessing's play *Nathan the Wise*, Tamao retorted, "Look, I don't need you to throw that radical stuff in my face. What do you take me for anyway?"

Nana fell silent. Countless beads of sweat clung to the tip of her nose. He couldn't tell which direction her eyes were looking in. A few seconds later, she started laughing like a glass bottle rolling down a concrete slope. There was definitely something strange about her. Remembering what his friend said about people who blew a fuse while they were studying abroad, Tamao cringed.

4

Amo loved the word "soul." At first he couldn't imagine what a "soul" could be although he sensed it must be different from things like walls or candles. Every time he heard the word his heart beat faster. In time, an oddly vivid image formed in his mind. The soul was an invisible mass of power that was always very near him—inside his chest, or perhaps wedged under his arm, or floating above his

Yoko Tawada

head—he couldn't tell exactly where, but it was there. And being there, it affected his feelings. When something he thought he'd never understand became crystal clear, he had his soul to thank for it; and if he was able to speak eloquently, it was because his soul was animated. His soul, though, didn't serve Amo. He was always the one who obeyed. If his soul told him to cry, he would immediately burst into tears. "The human soul is one kind of spirit. Spirits are living beings that cannot be seen and have a will of their own. They cannot describe this will with words, but we know by observation that it exists. Spirits have a purpose that they act toward. When this purpose is achieved, they are at rest." After writing this composition, Amo showed it to Petersen. Although impressed, the tutor couldn't see why his pupil had suddenly decided to write about such a topic, and asked if he had been reading some philosophical works that might have influenced him. When Amo told him this was something he had thought of himself, Petersen felt the unexpected appearance of words like "soul" and "spirit" in the boy's writing uncanny. Understood by no one, Amo continued to work on his compositions. His hunger for knowledge expanded and no one could suppress it. People found Amo's voice and the brightness of his face unsettling. When Petersen suggested that he be sent to university, and the Duke of Braunschweig agreed, no one was surprised. In June of 1727, Amo was sent to the town of Halle in Saxony as a student of philosophy.

When people saw Amo on the streets of Halle they stopped in their tracks, their eyes widening as if they were staring at the Devil. Some of the women screamed. In the little town of Wolfenbüttel, the baker's wife, the shoemaker, the farmer's wife who sold apples—everyone knew Amo, so no one stared at him. Familiarity allowed him to lead a normal life and forget how different he looked. But in Halle, he was painfully aware of the strangeness of his face in the eyes of the natives. He would be walking along a fence in an alley near the town square where the fountain was, and rocks would come flying. He initially thought it was children until he once peeked through a break in the fence and saw two men in ragged shirts glowering at him, each with a pile of stones clutched to his chest. When he went into a bakery, no matter how hungry he was, the baker would stand frozen and refuse to sell him anything. Some months later, when he transferred to the University of Wittenberg, nothing changed. This wasn't Amo's decision. The Duke, concerned about the heightening tensions between Prussia and Braunschweig, wanted him to move. It made no difference to Amo where he was. As long as he had a "father" to watch over him, one town was as good as another. He now lived in a lodging house for students. The landlady was stingy, though fortunately Amo didn't seem to frighten her, for she treated him just as she did the other students. They all had the same hard bread and milk in the morning, potato skins and soup with grease floating on the surface for lunch, and red wine with black bread spread with pork fat for supper. The landlady often told them with great pride that she was actually the daughter of a wealthy Portuguese family. She was raised surrounded by servants, including a number of African slaves who looked like Amo, she said, so far from upsetting her, the sight of his black face brought back nostalgic memories of her privileged childhood. After they lost their fortune, she traveled east with the husband her parents had chosen for her, but then he died, too, and she had been running this student lodging house ever since, though she was born into a great house with black slaves waiting on her—she repeated this story so many times that the students started doing amusing imitations of her. Black slaves. Wondering how he could have failed to see the huge tree standing in front of him, Amo slapped his forehead—a habit he'd picked up from Petersen. How could he have missed something so obvious? The ship was a slave ship. His father, his uncle, his brothers were captured and loaded onto it. But where were they taken? He remembered the many lands he had traveled through by carriage. Since leaving Amsterdam, he hadn't seen one black person. Where did they all go? Amo wanted advice about researching the slave trade but was afraid that if he asked, even the professors who had treated him kindly would see him differently once they realized his family were slaves. They might think him ungrateful. Here was the Duke of Braunschweig, paying for the education of a man who might have been a slave, and now that same man was planning to use the knowledge he received with the Duke's money to cast aspersions on the slave trade. His patron was supporting him not to waste his time on such matters, but to study philosophy. Herr Petersen said that the goal of philosophy was the moral perfection of human beings. Amo, however, didn't have a clear image of what the word "human" meant. People said that a human being possessed the ability to think. Yet no matter how complex a bird's thoughts might be, it was not human. When he asked a fellow student if a scullery maid was human, the student sneered and didn't reply. Another student explained with a lewd smile that for a human being to be born from a scullery maid's belly, she merely needed a human seed to produce the child so that even if the scullery maid were a horse she might give birth to a human baby. Undaunted, Amo posed the same question to one of his professors. After warning him against getting sidetracked by insignificant details, the man advised him to deal logically, and more severely, with the definition of "human" itself. The question, "Are black people on a slave ship human beings?" stayed on the tip of Amo's tongue.

Though Tamao spent most of his time cooped up in his room, his studies were not progressing well. When he opened the dusty old library books that he had borrowed, his mind wandered, leaving his eyes to vacantly skim the

Y O K O   T A W A D A

same page over and over again. He would walk down to the kitchen not so much out of hunger as from a vague desire to put something into his mouth. The landlady, hearing his footsteps, would emerge from her room. She was in her mid-sixties and extremely proud of having been to Japan, which her neighbors must have been sick of hearing about, for whenever she could, she would try to tell Tamao how she had seen the rock garden at Ryoanji and had bought a transistor radio at Akihabara. Tamao found it unbearable that people here saw him not as a student in the philosophy department, but above all as a Japanese. If his friend were to hear about this he would surely laugh and say, "Didn't I tell you not to bother going abroad? Europe will only get in the way of your studies."

Irritated, Tamao went outside for a walk only to run into Manfred, the man he'd met on his first day here. Manfred was in the process of crushing a cigarette underfoot, so perhaps he'd been standing there, waiting for Tamao to appear. The moment he saw Tamao he called out, "Hey there, Amo," with a sarcastic grin. After their first meeting, Tamao had immediately gone to the library where he discovered that Amo, brought here from Ghana in the eighteenth century, was the first African to be awarded a doctorate in philosophy from a European university, which was precisely why he couldn't forgive Manfred for calling him that name.

"Bet you're thirsty, aren't you?" Tamao retorted, trying to

sound tough. Apparently he succeeded, for Manfred gaped at him in surprise, then meekly nodded. "Come along then," Tamao said, assuming a casual air as he led the way into an upscale restaurant he'd been eyeing for some time. His old jacket hanging limply from his shoulders, Manfred followed. When he opened the menu, Tamao was disappointed to find the place cheaper than he'd expected. He ordered several hors d'oeuvres that looked expensive and were served in small portions. Tamao planned to keep Manfred cowed by acting like the last of the big spenders. He had money to spare as he had hardly bought anything since he arrived. Manfred soon grew very quiet.

When Tamao asked, almost angrily, "What kind of wine do you want?" Manfred replied in a tiny voice, "Your choice." Tamao knew his Italian wines, so he quizzed the waiter before deciding on one.

"I'm treating," he announced, feeling bolder. With his confidence turning to arrogance, he said, "I see you hanging around all the time—exactly what do you do for a living, anyway?" Cringing with fear, Manfred peered timidly up at Tamao, his mouth half open. No words came out, but his lips spluttered loudly. Alarmed, Tamao quickly added, "Not that it matters to me, of course." As soon as the hors d'oeuvres were arranged on the table—first a plate of eggplant, zucchini, red peppers and mushrooms, each gleaming with a faint sheen of oil, then slices of tomato and mozzarella, followed by foie gras—Manfred grabbed his knife

YOKO TAWADA

and fork. The words "God is . . . " escaped from his lips as he stuffed a piece of zucchini into his mouth, swallowing his sentence. He then started to say, "Things that pass away . . ." but quickly broke off a piece of bread and crammed it into his mouth as well. The trembling of his lips gradually subsided. With a wry smile, Tamao realized he was watching over Manfred like a nurse. Wiping the sweat from his forehead, Manfred drank some wine. By the time he finished his tortellini and polished off the last of the tiramisu, he seemed perfectly calm, and, smiling in spite of himself, Tamao remembered how "Pasta soothes the soul," in the words of a certain TV commercial. Then Manfred blurted out, "I'll treat you to Chinese sometime." Tamao automatically shook his head in refusal. Manfred looked puzzled. Tamao searched in vain for a good excuse. Didn't that foreign student Nana say she was working part-time in a Chinese restaurant? He would be lumped together with Nana and the other waitresses, reduced in Manfred's eyes to a mere speck in an Asian throng. He would have to dissuade Manfred.

"Don't you like Chinese food?" Manfred inquired.

"It's not that I don't like it, but my doctor has forbidden me to eat it." It was a peculiar lie. He hadn't seen Nana again since that first meeting, though the same night he had a dream about her. On the condition that she leave Wolfenbüttle, he was sleeping with her. "We can't have two people from the same country here at the same time, both studying Lessing," he told her. And she replied, "*You* can't—it doesn't bother *me* in the least." She was like an octopus's sucker, and try as he might, Tamao couldn't ejaculate. She drew him in and spat him out until he was gasping for breath, his belly hurt, and he wished for the end. But if he said something wrong, causing Nana to announce that she wasn't going to leave after all, he didn't know what he'd do. Tamao egged himself on. There's Manfred outside the window, green with envy, he told himself to keep from going limp. Professor Meyer's there with him—the pair of them wish they were me. At that very moment, a searing pain tore through his lower body, and Tamao woke up.

5

"The soul itself does not suffer," wrote Amo. "It appears to be in pain when a new connection forms, an invasion takes place, or a collision occurs. Still, it is not actually the soul that is suffering. Connection, invasion, and collision occur between the various parts, aspects, or elements within one existence," he continued. Since meeting Professor Johan Peter von Ludwig, Amo's passion for reading had increased. Professor Ludwig had a habit of lingering over the names of philosophers and their works when he spoke, savoring them like wine on the tongue. Perhaps that was why the books he recommended seemed to speak directly to Amo from the very first page. When Amo wrote papers of his own, though, he temporarily cleared his mind of the books he had read, rarely quoting from any of them. The words flowed smoothly from the tip of his pen. As he gazed at the quill, lost in thought, memories of birds would materialize. When he was a child, he observed every bird that flew past him, even noting the expression in its eyes. Now as he formed the letters on the page, the quill moved as if the spirit of the bird whose feathers had been plucked to make his pen were speaking. It wasn't Amo who wrote. It was the spirit of the dead bird.

Amo was so engrossed in his studies that he rarely went out. Professor Ludwig encircled his body like an invisible protective spirit, binding him to his books. The idea of a soul that did not feel pain comforted Amo. Even the stones people threw could not injure his soul. And, what's more, his soul was always present. Though friends might seem close, eventually they would depart. His fathers would also leave him someday. But as Amo moved from town to town, his soul would always travel with him. It had been with him since his childhood.

The only time his soul left him was at night, while he was asleep. With his soul no longer near, bad dreams were free to hurt him as much as they liked. Amo continued to have violent nightmares. The worst recurred again and again during what should have been the most memorable time of his life, when he was awarded a doctorate in philosophy. During the day he was showered with praise, surrounded by the proud faces of his professors and colleagues. Hoping to catch a glimpse of him, students would loiter outside his house early in the morning. Then at night when he closed his eyes, vaguely familiar men he couldn't see clearly ganged up on him and tied his hands and feet to a tree. With the tips of quill pens they stabbed the insides of his elbows, his thighs, his chest. Amo would be too shocked to speak. More from surprise than pain, his chest would almost burst. To avoid seeing who his attackers were he squeezed his eyes shut and moaned, bearing the pain until his moans grew so loud they woke him up, his back drenched in sweat.

Hounded by hunger, Tamao walked the streets until he finally stopped in front of the Chinese restaurant. There was only one in Wolfenbüttel, so he knew there was a good chance he'd bump into Nana. He shuddered at the thought. In the end, though, his longing for rice and soy sauce was too strong. Finding *ma-po-dou-fu* on the menu in pinyin and in Chinese characters, Tamao read off the four syllables in a monotone and then sat waiting, his eyes downcast to avoid seeing the faces of the waitresses walking by. With a platter of tofu drowned in spicy sauce in front of him, he forgot all about Nana, and when he paid the check and she still hadn't appeared, he decided she must have been fired, run out of money, and gone back to Japan.

He left the restaurant and was strolling back to his room

YOKO TAWADA

when he found himself in front of Lessing's house. He was marveling at the longevity of the cherry blossoms and their deep, rich hue when he heard a voice behind him: "So we meet again." Tamao cringed as if a policeman had ordered him to halt. He prayed that Nana didn't know he'd gone to eat *ma-po-dou-fu* on the sly.

"How are your studies coming along?"

She was carrying a wicker shopping basket filled with library books, their spines lined up neatly inside.

"Oh, so it's the girl radical who was spouting off about Lessing. . . . "

Tamao felt sure his sarcastic tone gained him the upper hand. With a pained expression as though someone had tried to yank her earlobe off, Nana launched into a diatribe about how as long as scholars continued to read the problem of sex in Lessing's work through the veil of idealized romantic love, they would remain blind to the pitfalls of 18th-century Enlightenment. Her spittle flew. "If you're still stuck on that old saw you've got a long way to go," Tamao interrupted, repeating a handy retort his friend often used, which didn't mean much but at least put the other person on the defensive. Nana's eyelashes twitched violently until she suddenly blurted out, "That means you must be . . . *MA-PO-DOU-FU!*" and burst out laughing. Her figure began to twirl like a windmill. His equilibrium destroyed, Tamao tried to say, "No I'm not," or "You've got it all wrong," but realized his voice was drifting farther and farther away. He knew he was talking. He just couldn't keep up with the continuous spray of words and lost all track of any meaning. Only when Nana grabbed his arm and shook him did the mechanical noise spurting from his mouth finally stop. He sighed with relief. When his speech ended, the scenery returned. Nana peered into his face with a worried look.

"I'm all right. It's really nothing at all," Tamao managed to whisper. He was afraid that if he spoke any louder, he would be spirited away by the sound of his own voice.

6

Amo didn't have much trouble getting a position at the University of Jena. He simply had to emphasize the fact that he was a young man from a poor family under the patronage of the Duke of Braunschweig, and permission was granted. Although poverty was hardly a shameful condition, Amo wondered how the authorities would react if they discovered his brothers had been sold as slaves.

"The aim of philosophy is the moral perfection of the mind and of the body," said Amo in his first lecture as Doctor of Philosophy. The people in the audience were drawn by different kinds of curiosity. Some were Orientalists, and thus interested in Africa as an exotic whole, while others merely wanted to see a black man at the podium. A serious-looking student of about twenty who was totally absorbed in Amo's lecture wanted to know what he meant by "the morality of the flesh." "Morality lies not only in the mind, but also in the body," Amo answered cautiously. No other philosopher had said this; it was an idea that had grown out of Amo's own experience. And because everyone's experience is different, arguments grounded in personal experience must be developed with great care. "For example, when you're about to throw a stone at a person or other living thing and your arm falters, or you feel pain in your heart, that is physical morality," Amo said. "Human beings who do not suffer in this way have not perfected their physical morality." He surveyed the audience but saw no reaction, only faces stacked like bricks. The student who had asked the question was no longer there.

Though Amo now rarely saw Professor Ludwig, he heard that he was sick. This man who had shielded him like a fur coat was growing more and more distant, and just as he was beginning to get used to the cold, the rumors of illness arrived, followed by the news of his death. Amo recalled Fraulein. She, too, had fallen ill and quickly vanished. Sobs rose from deep within his throat.

One night, Amo dreamed about Professor Ludwig. The professor looked like a doll kneaded from mud, and when the light struck him at certain angles, his face resembled that of different men. He didn't have eyes. Perhaps they still existed beneath the surface of his skin. Amo touched Professor Ludwig's cheeks, which really did feel like mud, his fingers sinking right into them. Then he woke up. In the morning, as he was walking through the university gate, a colleague hurried over, grabbed him by the arm, and whispered something in his ear. Although he couldn't make out what the man said, Amo sensed without having to ask that Professor Ludwig was dead. Instead of heading straight for his lecture, Amo walked along the dusty road. He wasn't sure where he was going. His soul followed, not far behind.

Tamao's studies still weren't progressing. He wanted to remain shut up in his room with his eyes riveted to his books. The walls frightened him, though, and when he was alone in his room, he broke into a cold sweat. One self could think, "I am here, now," and another self was capable of sensing his physical presence, but somebody who was no one at all had quietly slid a scalpel between the two. Without bothering to put on his jacket, Tamao left the house, pretending he was just stepping out for cigarettes. Once outside, walking the streets with studied indifference, he felt a little calmer. He passed the backs of strangers until he'd reached the outskirts of town, then turned right and continued on. When he saw a back he recognized, his pace quickened.

"Oh yeah? So what of it—I didn't make you any promises. That deal went bust all right, but I wasn't even there, so why don't you ask someone else what happened? You can't blame me for everything."

It was Manfred, mumbling to himself, fuming and sputtering. He was too engrossed in his monologue to notice Tamao walk up behind him, slightly to one side. Hesitating to speak, Tamao listened to him talk as if he were spitting out something foul while making excuses in a wheedling, whiny tone. When Tamao couldn't take anymore, he pummeled Manfred's meaty back. The man slowly turned around and stared straight at Tamao's nose with no sign of recognition. The appearance of those eyes, hard and as expressionless as marbles, startled Tamao so that he took a step back. Could these be "the eyes of one without a soul"? "Hey Manfred!" he shouted, much louder than he intended. This was the first time he addressed him this way. He would have preferred to use his surname—the unadorned Christian name was somehow embarrassing—but he felt that this was what was needed to bring Manfred's soul back. And in fact, after blinking rapidly a few times, in a startled voice Manfred uttered the syllables, "TA-MA-O." As his slack facial muscles tightened, his lips even managed a smile.

"What do you think you're doing standing here in the middle of the street?" Tamao demanded, but Manfred, apparently unaware that he'd been wandering around talking to himself, just stood there grinning.

"How about a drink?"

Side by side, the two set off. Manfred wobbled along, his pace fast then slow. Having to keep in step with his irregular gait irritated Tamao.

"You're worried about something, aren't you?" Tamao asked, putting on the big brother act. Manfred stared down at him in utter contempt and replied, "Amo, the likes of you could never understand what's bothering me." Clenching his fist, Tamao glowered at Manfred's fleshy jowls. They had come to the foot of a small bridge in an area the townspeople called Little Venice. Tamao pictured himself lunging at Manfred's side, pushing him straight into the water. Boy, would that feel good. Then he caught sight of Nana up ahead, walking toward them, waving both arms over her head. Like a kid in elementary school, Tamao returned the greeting. Manfred seemed to have forgotten all about Tamao and strolled on alone.

"Hey, wait up!" called Tamao, racing after him, but like a balloon carried off by the wind, Manfred's body receded farther and farther into the distance. "Hey, where're you going?!"

Tamao, in a daze, ran faster than he could ever remember. Manfred was floating away on a spring breeze. In time Tamao heard the approach of rhythmical footsteps and turned to see Nana beside him. He kept his pace, calling Manfred's name over and over again. When his breath was spent the name shattered and its fragments fell to the earth.

YOKO TAWADA

He was gasping, but with Nana by his side he couldn't stop now. How could she run so fast? Tamao was certain he had never reached this speed in his entire life. Manfred grew smaller and smaller. The stones beneath Tamao's feet rose from the ground and leapt before his eyes. Just when he thought he could go no further Nana stopped and bent at the waist, panting. Tamao looked back at her and stopped as well, breathing hard.

Though neither suggested it, they entered the nearest café, side by side.

"Two budding Lessing scholars running all over town chasing after a weird guy like that—rather droll, isn't it?" said Tamao, trying to sound scholarly, but Nana just laughed and said that she had decided to switch her research topic. Early in the eighteenth century there was an African philosopher who had studied here under the patronage of the Duke of Braunschweig, and eventually went on to get his doctorate, she started to tell him. . . .

7

When Amo's old servant fell ill, her daughter replaced her. Sometimes while cleaning a room, the younger woman would suddenly stop and stand motionless, staring vacantly into space. Or she would tenderly caress a book as big as a brick on Amo's desk. The neighbors said there was something odd about her. Amo often lost his temper in those days. When he flew into a rage, he would hurl his syllables through the air to wound his listeners' hearts. He didn't get angry at home, though, and always spoke to Marguerite—for that was her name—in soothing tones as if he were casting a spell on her. Nodding slightly, Marguerite would listen carefully to everything he said, although now and then she would throw him a spiteful glance for no apparent reason. She was always on the move: when her work in the kitchen was done she'd examine every corner of the house, dusting, polishing, picking up the carcasses of dead insects and tossing them out the window. Amo, who couldn't sit still either, would stride through the house, lost in thought, sailing between tables and chairs. Whenever he and Marguerite nearly ran into each other from opposite sides of the same piece of furniture, he'd burst into laughter. Amo had never been able to understand how his colleagues in the philosophy department managed to keep their hips and torsos so rigid when they walked. He certainly couldn't move that way. He observed them sitting in the library, submerged in their chairs like toads, and wondered if they were of the same species as himself. He knew Marguerite was, but those scholars could be beings from a different world. When Marguerite helped him put on his coat, their bodies would play a little game, swaying first right then left, or descend to the floor in a spiral motion, yet somehow she always got the garment on him. Marguerite saw that Amo's bottom was round and hard, and moved as if it had a life of its own. She watched his bottom as she held out his coat with both hands. Fully aware of this, Amo would give it a little twitch. Then he'd spin around to peer into her face, remembering how freely he'd played with women as a child. With the dramatic flourish of an actor, he'd plant a kiss on her cheek. She'd let out a squeal, but far from trying to escape, she'd stay glued to the spot still holding the coat, waiting for another surprise. One day Amo wanted her to run an errand and while looking for her behind the house, he overheard some women from the neighborhood gossiping around the washtubs. They were quizzing Marguerite about what Amo ate, whether his whole body was black, the size of his penis. He was always aware of their eyes watching him—in the shadow of a fence, behind the trees, from inside their houses. Yet whenever he approached and tried to speak to them, they looked terrified and ran away.

To Amo women were phantoms, formless as mist, floating up without warning from the depths of memory to caress his skin, only to disappear without telling him their names. But then one day, a woman who was all too real appeared before him. She was the eldest daughter of a noble family said to be related to the Russian aristocracy; they were introduced at a ball held at the Duke of Braunschweig's residence. When Amo saw her eyes, carved like diamonds, the air withdrew from his lungs. Those were the eyes of the women in the illustrated Bible stories he had learned his letters from as a child. The lady acted extremely reserved, for when spoken to she would only nod ever so slightly, or cover her mouth with her hand. Realizing that Amo was watching her, she looked his way from time to time with the hint of a smile on her lips. She's the embodiment of those Bible pictures, Amo repeated to himself. The folds in her evening gown seemed to express themselves far more delicately than the folds in other women's dresses, though even when her body moved, they remained perfectly still. The folds were trying to tell him something. Breathless, Amo clasped his hands over his ears.

Later that night, Amo had a bout of diarrhea and a fever. The next day he felt no better. He stayed in his room, and if he opened his books it wasn't to read but to pound them again and again with his fists, or caress the pages with sweaty hands, sighing all the while. He lost his appetite, and even the fat goose that Marguerite had used all her feminine wiles to persuade from the farmer was left untouched. Some days later, still dizzy from lack of sleep, Amo was on his way to his lecture when a carriage suddenly appeared, barreling straight for him. He managed to stumble over to the side of the road; the driver raised his whip, showering him with curses. A face peered out at the fracas. It soon retreated, though not before he saw that it belonged to the Russian lady. For one brief moment, she stared straight at him.

His fever turned from bad to worse. The entrance to his stomach closed, and he couldn't eat a thing. When someone spoke to him he tried to listen but a different voice flitted around his face like a fly, and though he could feel the other person staring at him in disbelief, he simply couldn't continue the conversation. To Marguerite's worried inquiries he could only answer that he thought something must be wrong with his stomach. If this obsession continued he would be trapped in an emotional cul-de-sac, and there was no telling what might happen next. Amo decided to write her a letter. The late Professor Ludwig had praised his handwriting, so he had nothing to worry about in this respect. He was confident in his literary style as well. After all, he wrote poetry. When he dipped his pen in the inkwell, a calm passed over him. After the first word he wrote, "Dear . . ." he thought he saw his alter ego in both the shaky lines and the bold sweeps of the pen, and his heart beat faster. "Dear . . ." "Dear . . ." He wrote the word over and over again but he could go no further. Even though he knew the lady's name, he was afraid to write it down. Once he did, he felt his secret would be known to the entire world. When her name was finally on the paper, he was faced with the problem of the opening line. "In meditative wisdom the totally awakened mind tirelessly seeks the foundations of knowledge, and nobly . . .," he wrote, and then realized that this was not a love letter. It was the soul he must write about, not the mind. Surely the young lady must have a soul, too, he thought, but this intensified his worries. For what if her soul left her body at night to fly around town, and was captured by bad dreams?

"I constantly pray that your soul stays with you, day and night," Amo wrote. Unable to think of anything else to say, he signed his name and put the letter in an envelope. Though Marguerite delivered most of his messages, he could hardly entrust her with this one. There were no friends he felt he could rely on, either. He decided to sneak into her mansion late at night and hand it to her himself. If they were the only ones in the room, it would remain their secret. A chill crawled up the back of Amo's neck. He could see quite well in the dark. He never fell down and skinned his nose after a late night drinking in a tavern the way his colleagues did. There was a garden behind the lady's house with a wall around it that looked easy enough to scale. Thinking only of the moment when he'd be standing before her, he wore his best trousers, and unable to spread his legs far enough apart, he nearly fell from the top of the wall. The letter was safe in his breast pocket. He patted it twice for good luck before sneaking across the garden. A candle flickered in the second-story window. If he stood atop the railing at the back door, he would be able to reach the balcony. Then he'd only have to pull himself up. He peered into the kitchen through a tiny window around back, but it was pitch-black and he couldn't see anything. Balancing himself on top of the railing, he was cautiously reaching for the balcony when he heard the sound of a wild beast running through the grass behind him. Instinctively, he twisted around and was about to jump down when a club struck him hard below the knees. With a high-pitched scream, Amo fell to the ground. Since he had rounded his back, he felt no pain when he rolled onto the grass, but before he could get up, a man stood over him, hitting him with a club. A kick in the belly brought a bitter-tasting liquid up his throat, a blow to the nose started the blood flowing, and a punch in the jaw pushed his face into the mud as his spine was beaten like a washing board.

If that had been all, Amo might have recovered fully after a long rest. But when he heard from Marguerite that the whole town was talking about how he had tried to attack the young lady in her bedroom, he took to his bed. The lady herself was wailing that the incident had cast a blemish on her life from which she would never recover. Amo felt that his soul was about to set out on a long journey away from the land of the Bad Spirits.

A year after Amo left for the African continent, his love story was being performed as a wildly popular puppet drama. A shadowy character named Hans was turning real-life incidents into outrageous spectacles that drew huge crowds. In Hans's version, Amo was a lion who escaped from the jungle, and drooling profusely as he tried to seduce the young lady, she ran away shrieking. A huge tongue drooped wantonly from the lion's mouth like a banana. The sight of the tongue made the audience laugh until they choked. Fortunately, Amo was no longer there. Marguerite saw him off, and the following day returned to the village of her birth. The young lady spent some time in bed with a fever. Upon her recovery, she set out for the home of distant relatives in Russia.

IN FRONT OF TRANG TIEN BRIDGE

One day a letter with a strangely alluring stamp the color of a cock's comb was delivered to Minamiyama Kazuko. The paper inside, folded into a tight square, crackled like radio static when she forced it open. The letters on the page were finely etched, faded as a fresco on a wall long exposed to the elements, and as she struggled to make each one out Kazuko grew more curious about who had written them than what they said. The harder she looked the dimmer the handwriting became until finally she noticed the return address.

It was a mesmerizing word slashed out in bold strokes with a magic marker onto a crude handmade sign that was propped precariously in a corner on the college campus. More than a country's name, it was rage itself in graphic design, and because Kazuko feared politics like a disease, a curtain lowered in her mind whenever she saw it. She would veer off to one side to avoid the word, but it would always be too late. A student in a polo shirt the color of withered grass would jump out from behind the sign with a wide-open mouth. The girl who started expounding on "the kou-sei hanminh of mailan" would be a boy by the time the part about "we must konsen the meiroku of hantaku" came around. Whenever hordes of students with narrow hips, trembling fingers, vacant eyes, and androgynous flat shoes were hounding Kazuko with Chinese characters, the enig-matic word, *Vietnam*, would always appear on a sign nearby.

There was no reason why Kazuko should be receiving a letter from Vietnam. A friend from college used to teach Japanese at a university in Hué, but she was back in Tokyo now. And besides, her name was not Hisayama Mika. Since Kazuko didn't know anyone by that name, it was Vietnam that filled her mind and drove her heart farther and farther south across its border. The name Champa had once slipped out of the pages of a World History textbook and tumbled straight into her pocket. But she no longer owned the book and couldn't even remember which Chinese char-acters formed the word. Chanting *Champa, Champa . . .* brought back the delicious feeling of release she felt when she passed her entrance exams and threw her old textbooks away, though the college she had studied so hard to get into she dropped out of long ago.

There was nothing to do but read Hisayama Mika's letter. "I was so happy to get your postcard. I think it's wonderful that you're making a name for yourself as a jour-nalist in Europe—a continent so near and yet so far. I, myself, found nothing in Paris. I ended up traveling all the

YOKO TAWADA

way to Hué with a Vietnamese friend. Please come visit me if you like."

Kazuko remembered a red curtain, a dark dusty corner behind the curtain, the stench of old running shoes, so worn they were about to fall apart. The place was suddenly so close she could have been there yesterday. In Paris, covering an international dance festival, an Asian girl crying backstage. The girl was in her mid-twenties, had squarish eyes, and though her jeans looked brand-new, there hardly seemed to be legs or hips inside them. They talked during the half hour it took to set up the lighting for the rehearsal, and ended up exchanging addresses. So that was Hisayama Mika, Kazuko thought, and at the same moment the name Cambodia materialized in her mind. Once, in a dream, a person with a megaphone for a mouth repeatedly screamed this country's name at her, nailing her to the spot where she stood in front of a train station. Instead of a stomach, the figure had a box with a slot for coins. Crying for help, Kazuko yelled *Champa! Champa!* over and over again. She often had similar dreams, like trying in vain to catch a train on the Yamanote line. If I can't get on here I'll get on at the next station, she'd think to herself, but when she arrived she'd see a sign for Laos. It was a name she had never heard before.

"If you ever go back to Japan, why not stop in Hué on the way? It's only an hour by plane from Ho Chi Minh City. If you do come, there's someone I want you to meet. She's majoring in physics at the university, and she looks exactly like you, Kazuko. If I said you two were identical twins, I'm sure everyone would believe me," Hisayama Mika wrote.

Kazuko had no memory of bumping into another lump of flesh in the womb. Here in Berlin, however, there seemed to be twins everywhere she looked. She saw twins asleep in double baby carriages, and Vietnamese twins holding the left and right hands of their German foster mother. Kazuko couldn't imagine herself as one of such a pair. She retrieved the enormous world atlas from the shelf and opened it on her desk. China filled the whole left side of the Asian page, while the color of the sea covered most of the right. The fluorescent light reflected off the shiny surface of the map, making it impossible to read any of the countries' names. The day before, she interviewed a Mr. Ohsawa, a former music student, in the sushi bar he recently opened. Showing her an inside-out roll, he said, "See? Rice doesn't need to be wrapped in seaweed; the grains stick together just fine even when on the outside. The nori stays curled up inside." She slipped a copy of *Writing on the Wall Without the Wall*, the complementary newspaper piled up on the counter, into her bag. Apparently, the newspaper was published by the Japanese community in Berlin, though Kazuko had never heard of it before. Here, too, she found the word *Vietnam*. "Recently neo-Nazi and other right-wing groups have been brutally attacking the Vietnamese. To avoid cases of mistaken identity, we Japanese must always wear glasses and neckties. Women should put on as much jewelry as possible, and be sure to carry a brand-name handbag. And let's all be careful never to use the subway or other forms of public transportation."

The inside-out roll does not let the teeth penetrate the paper-like texture of nori first before chomping into plump, sticky rice. Hard enamel quickly sinks through the soft white grains to encounter a chewy wad of seaweed so tough it seems like a will that can never be broken.

Kazuko thought of going to Vietnam two years earlier, but her passion for travel wasn't strong enough at the time. Wandering through a luggage sale in a department store she was more likely to picture herself sitting with one butt cheek resting on a suitcase in a corner of her room as she stared into space, than actually carrying one. Though she might have traveled somewhere to cover a story at the instigation of her editor, she wouldn't have simply set out on a whim. Now her travel fever was a serious infection. It made her buy airline tickets with money she couldn't spare, emptying her savings account, and the long-forgotten name Ho Chi Minh reverberated in her ears. Kazuko's fingers seemed too long and too thin to her, so as she put her hands on her desk she instinctively curled them under. Perturbed by the smallness of her feet, she always wore pointed shoes.

"The German lit. people are getting together for yosen-abe next Friday. You want to come?" a foreign student named Kaneda asked Kazuko over the phone. Bristles of beard sprouted in the breaks between his words. Kazuko answered automatically, "I can't. I'll be traveling," but realizing that the word "traveling" sounded so affected it was almost funny, she quickly added, "Sightseeing." "Exactly where are you going?" he inquired confidently. "To Southeast Asia." To be more specific and say, "Vietnam," would have been embarrassing, like letting him in on a secret. "What? And when did you decide that?" Kaneda asked heatedly, as if he couldn't forgive Kazuko for having made up her mind without consulting him. You'd think we were married, she mused with a wry smile. They were neither lovers nor even close friends.

I'm a member of the tourist race, thought Kazuko. Tourists will go anywhere without being asked. They can get interested in anything and forget everything as soon as their trip is over; they'll skip meals to buy train tickets, return home whining that they're so tired they'll never take another trip ever again, and the following day have their maps spread out, wondering where to go next.

While shopping in Wilmersdorfer Strasse the following day, Kazuko stopped at a travel agency to reserve a seat on a flight to Ho Chi Minh City. A big-breasted woman, planted firmly in front of the flower shop next door, brandished a bunch of green stems at her. Kazuko felt an itch between her fingernails and the flesh underneath. She had to get to Vietnam. When she asked, "Can you get me a visa?" the travel agent adjusted his glasses and inquired cautiously, "Do you need one?" He's mistaken me for a Vietnamese going home for a visit, Kazuko thought, but she couldn't quite bring herself to say, "Yes, because I'm Japanese." How could she claim to be Japanese when she wasn't wearing a single piece of jewelry or even carrying a brand-name handbag? she asked herself, nearly cracking up. If there was a Vietnamese woman called Ms. A returning home, it would have been easier to imagine herself being Ms. A. "I don't have Vietnamese citizenship so I need a visa," she explained. "Are you a German citizen?" Perhaps the man thought she was a war orphan some German couple had adopted, on her way to see her native country for the first time. "So, you have German citizenship, do you?" the travel agent queried again. "No, I do not have German citizenship. I also do not have Vietnamese citizenship. I need visa." Say there was a Japanese woman called Ms. B whose grammar crawled out the window whenever she got mad. That woman might very well be Kazuko.

Kazuko couldn't say for sure whether or not she dreamed in color. She didn't think dreams had smells. Nevertheless, she recently had a very smelly dream. Some part of her body—she couldn't tell exactly which—was spread out like a loaf of Turkish flatbread. The tail, eyes, and guts of a fish were buried in this flesh-bread. The whole thing looked rotten, and even if it wasn't, it was repulsive: the carcass of a fish torn to pieces, then stuffed into a lump of human meat. She could neither believe that the bread belonged to her, nor give it a name.

"I've decided to go to Vietnam. I'll be away for about three weeks, so could you look after my cat while I'm gone?" Kazuko asked her friend Marianne. Though she didn't mind taking care of the animal, Marianne had no idea what to do with Vietnam, this new country Kazuko had suddenly thrust upon her. "You'll be going to Japan, too, won't you?" Marianne asked somewhat resentfully. After finally making Japan sound like a real place, Kazuko had no right to confuse her this way by bringing up a different name altogether. "Why go to Japan? It's 3,000 kilometers away from Vietnam, you know." Like a thief stomping boldly around her room, knowing her stolen antiques are safely hidden in the basement below, Kazuko added hotly, "Do you how far that is? If you started in Berlin, you'd wind up in the middle of Africa." This had as much effect on Marianne as a swat on the cheek from a child's balloon. Why talk about thousands of kilometers when Asia was all in the same place? Marianne asked another question, one Kazuko was sick of hearing: "But don't you get homesick?" "Not for Japan I don't. It's the Pacific Ocean I miss," she replied, and immediately a chill of disgust ran down her spine. Pacific—this word that popped out of her mouth without thought—sounded terribly pathetic. Willfully crying its eyes out, the Pathetic Ocean crossed border after border on its journey southward.

Kazuko was supposed to change planes in Paris and catch an Air France flight to Ho Chi Minh. The morning of her departure, however, the news on the radio said that the electricity was down in Paris due to a general strike. Kazuko pictured the airport in the midst of a blackout. The ground crew signaling the flight crew by waving flaming torches above their heads. Trailing streaks of light behind them, the fires would float through the darkness like the glowing souls one sometimes sees in graveyards. Kazuko took out a notebook and started writing a song: "In a pitch-black plane, by candlelight, stewardesses give all the bread they have to hungry passengers. Each piece is frozen, an egg-shaped piece of ice within." Besides the notebook she used for stories and interviews, she had a special one for songs. If there were a Ms. C, a former budding singer-song-writer who in junior high school spent her nights with an acoustic guitar hugged tightly to her chest and her days scribbling chords in the margins of her textbooks, then Ms. C was almost certainly Kazuko. Much to Ms. C's surprise, the Paris airport was ablaze with lights. International flights were leaving on schedule. The aluminum foil covering the steak the stewardess served her was so hot that Kazuko instinctively jerked her hand away and banged her funny bone on the armrest. Her elbow went numb, the warmth draining from her arm. A spot of steak sauce stained her white blouse. Both gas and electricity were supposed to be out because of the strike, so why was the food so hot? Kazuko was getting mad. Not to be outdone, the steak bubbled in its grease. Gripping the small but surprisingly heavy knife, Kazuko stabbed the meat hard, right in the center. Sauce spurted out to form a fresh blot on her blouse. France had started testing atomic weapons again, and here she was using their national airline. The plane left Europe wrapped in a blanket of snow; an expanse of white shrank beneath her. From the capital of France, the atomic weapons tester, she was flying to a former French colony. Just another dumb tourist with no other way to get to Vietnam, she murmured to herself as if she were talking about someone else.

The air in Ho Chi Minh was very heavy, and the heat completely opened her pores. She climbed into the backseat of a taxi. Up ahead, a swarm of motorbikes swarmed toward her. Viewed from the front, they looked like grasshoppers. There was tension in the riders' chins. Young men with straight eyebrows and lips lifted slightly at the edges in a smile; women with slender cheeks and unflinching eyes. She wondered why Japanese faces looked so puffy and powdery. Perhaps too many cabbage patches had been paved over. Maybe white cabbage butterflies in search of their vanished vegetables wandered into dreams and fluttered their wings above the sleepers' faces, powder sprinkling down and sticking permanently to cold, damp skin.

Motorbikes welled up from the earth and one by one

slipped past Kazuko. A woman would sometimes be riding with another woman perched behind her. Bike after bike glided by in the dripping heat. If a man were driving, another man, or a woman, or a mother and child would be riding with him. Small vehicles carrying families of four looked like animals on wheels. Black hair streaming out in the humid evening air, shirtsleeves flapping in the wind, bare feet clinging to sandals. In Germany even children on bicycles wore helmets, but no one bothered to here. The traffic moved at such a leisurely pace it seemed on the verge of stopping. Kazuko didn't realize how slowly her taxi was going until they entered the city.

A member of the tourist race, Kazuko was always in a hurry at home and marveled at the slowness of life in the places she visited. HERE TIME HAS STOPPED, the travel posters would say, and always in the background a photo of the sky taken who knows where—Greece, or India, or China perhaps. "Here for a vacation?" the taxi driver asked. Kazuko planted her bottom, which she had raised slightly off the seat, firmly back down. She had been about to take off her stockings, which were stuck to her sweaty inner thighs. The driver's head was the shape of a well-formed apple, and covered with shiny, neatly trimmed black hair. He looked about sixteen, though he might have been as old as twenty. The back of his shirt was a dazzling white, without a single wrinkle. It made Kazuko want to hide her clammy legs. "There are lots of children in Vietnam," the driver said enthusiastically, offering no further explanation as he maneuvered skillfully among the motorbikes with a business-like ease. "Are there many traffic accidents?" Kazuko fired back without trying to make a logical connection. "There are when Vietnam wins a soccer match. Everyone drives like crazy all over the city," replied the driver, and Kazuko realized with some dismay that, when spoken aloud, *kô tsû jiko*, the Japanese term for traffic accident, didn't bear the least resemblance to a collision between two motor vehicles. In fact, it sounded as though it should mean something more like "sheep bones thrown away in a grassy field."

Japanese motorbikes were slender and rather cute, while the ones manufactured in the Czech Republic were heftier and all the same drab brown. The Vietnamese straddling these foreign bikes, though slight, looked strong all the way down to their fingertips. There was nothing helpless about them. The smiles of Vietnamese in Berlin, even their way of moving, tended to arouse pity. They walked as though they weren't quite sure their hips would agree to move with their thighs. Their dark eyes darted right and left, careful not to meet anyone's gaze, watching out for danger. Kazuko was like that, too. In Berlin, whenever she saw something moving nearby, she'd scurry out of the way. She stuck to the corners to keep from stealing anyone's space. She was always spying around, frightened of what might be coming.

The souvenir shops on Dong Khoi Street were lined up like a row of front teeth. A glossy sheen that caught

Kazuko's eye, reminding her of the hard, plastic clipboard she had used in primary school, turned out to be a tray. Embedded in the tray were shiny seashells of seven different colors. The shells were arranged to form what appeared to be a rearing horse with its mane spread out in a tangle, then Kazuko realized that it was a dragon. A girl of about fifteen ran out calling, "Hallo! Hallo!" There's something sad about souvenirs. The child's face was cheerful yet serious. She sells this depressing junk every day, so why haven't the tourists' shoes left prints on her face? Kazuko wondered, remorse billowing inside her. Like a sparrow in flight, the little vendor fluttered over the mountain of knickknacks to where Kazuko was standing. But Kazuko wasn't seeing the things in her shop. It was as if the stacks of trays, the rows of dolls dressed in sedge hats and nylon ao dai were not even there. Or as if she knew exactly where everything was without looking. The girl shoved a doll with Barbie eyes into Kazuko's hand. Struggling to shake off her embarrassment, Kazuko twisted her body left and right. Kitsch was a word she hated, and would never use. Yet this Vietnamese Barbie doll was so frightening she wanted to shut her eyes, and could only imagine the word kitsch to describe its vulgarity. Suddenly, she was disgusted with Kazuko, standing in front of this souvenir shop tossing around abstract concepts like kitsch. "Tell me," she chided, "what's wrong with a Vietnamese Barbie doll anyway?" The Kazuko on the receiving end couldn't think of an answer, and was beginning to feel terribly guilty. She escaped from this shop only to walk past another just like it. Still another nearly identical one waited further along. If she stopped, a girl would come flying out. Kazuko shook her head. It wasn't that she was merely determined not to buy anything—all the cheap trinkets were starting to look like cancer cells. "But why are *they* so malignant? The tourists are the real carcinoma, aren't they?" Another unanswerable question. No one around to ask it, but she heard it anyway. If we were to call the disgruntled owner of that voice Ms. D, then Ms. D might have raised the corners of her eyes like fishhooks and continued: "It's arrogant of you to despise souvenirs this way. And saying they depress you is sentimental. You claim to be sad because you think you're above the realities of the situation. If you really hate this stuff so much, then why not be honest, look the girl in the eye, and tell her you hate the shit she's hawking, that it makes you sick just to look at it?" The moment she stopped walking, another voice would call, "Hallo! Hallo!" so she hurried on. As long as she was moving, the oily veneer of souvenirs would slide past her like the wind. Then she glimpsed someone she thought she recognized, a woman polishing a tray with a dry white cloth. Startled, she began to wonder if that woman's face hadn't been identical to her own. But she couldn't turn around and go back for another look. Souvenirs are . . . worthless? . . . lovely? . . . cheap? . . . cute? . . . ugly? What if she were just being silly, and it was, in fact, possible to create aesthetic harmony by attaching vinyl to bamboo, or metal to tofu?

"Arrogant if you're sad, lazy if you're not," Kazuko sang to herself as she turned the corner and sat down at a restaurant in front of a construction site. It was called the Big Pup Cup, though Kazuko couldn't imagine what that might mean. While waiting for the waiter to bring a menu, she read the scene before her as though it were a cartoon, beginning with the upper right-hand frame. "I'm arrogant so I'm not sad," she sang. The melody was beginning to sound maudlin, like an overplayed pop song. A bat flew restlessly overhead, following a course unrelated to either a circle or a straight line. Homo sapiens were busy building a mammoth hotel below. The barricade around the construction site plastered with KEEP OUT signs reminded Kazuko of the Shinjuku district in Tokyo when she was growing up during the 1960s. Leaning against the barricade was a young girl holding a box filled with the bottles of juice she was selling. A boy of six or seven with a cloth sack hanging around his neck was chatting with her. When a young French couple sat down at the next table, he pattered over to them. Sidling up to the man, he took some postcards out of his sack and flipped through them one by one with slender fingers that seemed too long for the rest of his body. Absorbed in their menus, this couple clearly wasn't buying. The boy then dashed out to the main street where three Asian women who appeared to be Japanese stood gawking. Their makeup, the color of drawing paper, was so thick it gave their cheeks a powdery look; they were smartly dressed in clothes with invisible seams. Kazuko looked for one of her notebooks to jot down a list of the physical characteristics that make Japanese women look Japanese, but realizing she had left them both at the hotel, she took out her guidebook instead. She would write some notes in the margin and copy them out later. As soon as he spied the guidebook, however, the little postcard seller scurried over. "You Japanese? No Vietnam?" he asked breathlessly, repeating the question over and over, grinning like a windmill. Oh, so he didn't bother with me before because he thought I was Vietnamese, Kazuko thought, finally understanding. There was a ballpoint pen in the side pocket of her bag along with a subway ticket from Berlin. "The Japanese," she wrote, "are people carrying guidebooks written in Japanese."

A little girl in sandals played nearby, hopping on one foot. Like a monstrous beetle, a car inched along. A cyclo sped past the car. There was no one on foot. Walking, apparently, was a peculiar activity. People here hopped, pedaled bicycles, straddled motorbikes, sat on chairs or the floor, or stretched out on the earth. But they didn't walk.

In Shinjuku, everyone walked, keeping the same rhythm, forming a current strong enough to sweep skyscrapers off their foundations and carry the entire city away. Moving their legs like scissors. A bit like soldiers. As they'd practiced in junior high school. Left, right, left, right. Marching through Shinjuku, she often thought of war. Sharp corners crumbling, causing whole buildings to cascade down. Tremors wracking the town until something completely different shot up from the rubble; crowds parading quietly through a metropolis turned into a monster.

Slices of eel floated in her coconut milk curry. The waitress looked exactly like Tanabe Mayumi, a woman she had once stayed with in Osaka. The way Ms. Tanabe filled the creases and hollows of your body with soothing words gave the impression that she was trying to sell you something even when she wasn't. You had to imitate her at least a little or you'd feel out of place, ungainly as an elephant's leg. Flustered, Kazuko spilled her soup. Here she was, playing the elephant's leg to the waitress's peahen crest. It was too awful for words. Having given the coconut Kazuko had just started to sip a shake and declared, "There's nothing left in this," when there clearly was, the waitress proceeded to ask, "You'll have more rice, won't you?" and brought it before Kazuko had a chance to answer. Finally, jabbing the center of the menu she commanded, "Try this for dessert." This is what it meant to sell. Selling was service. She would serve Kazuko until Kazuko was roasted and ready to be served up fresh from the oven.

Kazuko was furious that the waitress shook her coconut. Not because the top of its head was cut off. The milk inside felt like it flowed from her own heart. Before she even tasted it, the milk quickened the core of her brain. And what about the fruit she ordered, not because she wanted dessert but so they wouldn't think she was stingy? Tourists are forced to keep up appearances. No matter how hard they try to seem benevolent, everything they do inevitably looks bad, leaving them burdened with guilt. This dulls their thinking. "What kind of fruit would you like for dessert?" "Coconut will be fine." "Coconut is not for dessert. Let me make another choice for you." She meekly acquiesced. The waitress brought out a fruit Kazuko had never seen before. Though shaped like a kiwi it was brick red, and tasted like chocolate ice cream.

On the way back to her hotel, Kazuko took a slight detour to pass by the Rex Hotel. In the middle of an intersection, she saw an island rimmed with concrete and with real trees growing on it. A wave of motorbikes swirled around the island, the tide swelling, ebbing, and occasionally breaking as a group of bikes accelerated. In the center was a peaceful oasis. You might call this a park, thought Kazuko. Hundreds of aluminum balloons shaped like manju cakes tied to the vendors' bicycles drifted in the deep blue sky. "Sell balloons all day, night falls come what may," Kazuko tried chanting to herself but suddenly found her little song embarrassing and crumpled it up inside her head. Two teenage girls with coconuts dangling from poles slung over their shoulders rushed up to her. Each was carrying four coconuts in front and four in back, and when they came to a halt their bodies continued to gently sway. They stood waiting for the swaying to subside as if anticipating a moment of awakening. Then, with what looked like a solemn bow, they simultaneously lowered their poles to the ground. Absorbed in the girls' behavior, Kazuko didn't realize that someone had snuck up behind her. Feeling something the size of a soccer ball brush her cheek, she turned to see a mellow-looking middle-aged man. He, too, was holding a coconut, and then thrust it toward her, the straw sticking out of the top of the coconut almost touching her nose. When she shook her head violently, the man gave up and sauntered off. The girls stared after him until he was too far away to see them pointing at him, and said in Japanese, "No good." It sounded like they were trying to warn her against eating him. Then one of the girls offered Kazuko a coconut and announced, "This one's good, Big Sis," with the other following suit. A clump of jet-black hair, drenched with sweat, was plastered to the first girl's tanned forehead. There was plenty of skin on these cheeks and brows to soak up the sun's rays. Their faces and the slightly husky tone of their voices filled Kazuko with nostalgia. Tourists often wax nostalgic over things they are seeing for the first time. "Good taste. One dollar," they chimed in unison, shooting their index fingers straight up at the sky with the word "one." "Buy mine, Big Sis." Kazuko was embarrassed to be called Big Sis. Surely it wasn't appropriate for this situation, she thought, but then again, what was wrong with it? And what exactly did they mean, anyway? Waves of laughter drained Kazuko's strength until she couldn't even giggle anymore, though her body still trembled. "Good taste," repeated the girl with the bangs. Her eyes never moved. The name Kana dawned on Kazuko. This child was Kana, and she, Kazuko, was about to drain a coconut of its bodily fluid. But no name she could think of suited the other girl, and besides, wouldn't buying from only one of them leave a blemish, like a spot of spilled ink, on the bond between the two girls? If there was a certain Ms. E, constantly worried about the hidden tides of malice and resentment that rise and fall between strangers, then Kazuko was determined to slam the door in Ms. E's face. She would not let uncertainty keep her from being drawn in whichever direction the current pulled her. So when someone said, "Good taste," and her mouth filled with fruity saliva, she would devour the nearest coconut. As she intended to nod, however, her head must have slipped to one side, making it seem that she'd snubbed the child, who promptly chirped, "OK?" once more for good measure. "OK, Big Sis? OK. I'll get a knife." Kazuko blushed and looked down. The girl borrowed a rusty carving knife from a man selling Coca-Cola and soon returned, slashing the coconut twice, left and right. Slipping a straw into the new hole, she handed the coconut to Kazuko. Meanwhile, the other girl placed her hands on Kazuko's knees and shook them gently, pleading, "Big Sis, tomorrow, tomorrow." Apparently she wanted Kazuko to buy *her* coconut the next day. Kazkuo's guilt washed away; it was a relief to repeat,

"Tomorrow," with a decisive nod this time. The child then stuck out her pinky, singing, "Promise on your finger," to which Kazuko could only respond by offering her own, which was much too long, while wondering how this Vietnamese girl could have learned a Japanese children's ritual. And then Kazuko remembered she really couldn't keep her promise after all. "The day after?" she tried, but the girl just tilted her head and looked puzzled. "Tomorrow" she understood, but "the day after" was a complete mystery. And besides, once you promised on your little finger there could be no "day after." For if you broke tomorrow's promise you'd have to swallow a thousand sharp needles and the day after wouldn't matter anymore. While Kazuko handed a dollar bill to the coconut girl, the "promise" girl intoned, "Don't tell a lie." As a member of the tourist race, Kazuko knew that as long as she was speaking broken English she could tell any number of lies. The girl had seen right through her, and that's why she had hooked her pinky around Kazuko's: "Promise on your finger / If you lie I'll make you drink / A thousand needles in a wink / By our pinkies linked."

Coconut milk is like fluid undulating deep in the inner ear as it picks up sounds from the outside. Kazuko recently read something about the auditory sense having been created by water. If the liquid in your ears dried up, you would no longer hear. "Cock-and-bull, shuttlecock, half-crocked, three in a muddle, laughing from a puddle," Kazuko sang to herself. The two girls sat beside her, one on each side, their eyes about to be absorbed into the darkness of the night. Perhaps they weren't as anxious to make a profit as she'd thought; they didn't even try hawking their wares to bespectacled men with cameras around their necks. Kazuko sipped at her coconut. You can't tell from the outside whether there's a lot of milk in a coconut or just a little, but if you drink slowly because you're afraid to finish too fast, the milk seems to last forever. The girls were sixteen and had worked as street vendors for nearly five years now, ever since finishing school. Though slim as boys, their cheeks were plump and their eyes sparkled so that when they laughed they could have been twelve. It occurred to Kazuko that she might be seeing them through the same eyes as the people in Berlin who saw her and always thought she looked so young. The light turned green and a herd of motorbikes took off with a mechanical roar. "Big Sis is . . . twenty-five?" The question brought Kazuko back to herself. These kids, too, took ten years off her age. The natural accumulation they expected the years to leave on a face must be missing from hers. And they in turn lacked what Kazuko had been taught to see as maturity.

There were always cyclos parked in front of the hotel. The drivers, vaguely taunting, yet eager for business, watched her walk in and walk out again. When she returned in the evening, they quietly observed. But as soon as she stepped outside and started down the street in the morning,

YOKO TAWADA

the barrage of "Cyclo! Cyclo!" rained down with such force that their voices seemed like hands reaching out to grab her. Whenever Kazuko rode instead of walked, she felt as if the earth had been stolen from beneath her feet. If a certain Ms. F liked to stroll along the shore for hours without hearing human voices, on what she considered a small excursion within a larger journey, Kazuko was also Ms. F. Why, then, did she choose Vietnam rather than another jaunt to Norway? Lots of people never go anywhere on vacation except Scandinavia. They return again and again to the beauty they know.

But as far as she could tell, no one walks far in Ho Chi Minh City. Seated in a cyclo, Kazuko searched in vain for pedestrians. Instead, she saw people pedaling bicycles, men squatting on the ground repairing sewing machines, whole families on motorbikes, women stirring vats of soup, their faces bathed in the rising steam. Sitting in a cyclo made her feel like a pile of dirt scooped up by a bulldozer. The driver's feet were covered with a layer of dust—an outer hide, perhaps, to protect the skin beneath. His seat was so high up that when she turned around she was eye level with his crotch. The street was crowded but the cyclo slipped along with the lightness of a whirligig beetle skimming across the surface of the water, somehow managing to avoid its kin. The wind brushed her face like a caress. There were no streetlights, so no Walk/Don't Walk commands. The frogs and beetles could move freely across the pond. Red plastic basins and chairs in the shops floated in and out of her field of vision and looked like toys. She remembered squatting in a sandbox clutching a shovel the same shade of red, and without warning, a hot liquid spilled out from between her thighs, making the sand bubble and turn dark.

In the photograph, an American GI holds the upper half of a Vietnamese soldier's severed body in one hand like an old rag. The head of the Vietnamese soldier still has eyes, a nose, a mouth. The GI seems to be smiling. There's no one in the War Museum, thought Kazuko. I'm not here either, that's why it's perfectly silent, a world too far beyond for sound to reach my eardrums. With the breath crushed out of her, she came to her senses and gulped in air. She was definitely in the War Museum, standing in front of a photograph, sensing people around her. The caption noted that a Japanese photographer had taken it. Kazuko gritted her teeth, clinging to her patriotism, hoping that neither the blond youth beside her, nor the one next to him, whose face she couldn't see, nor any of the others looking at this image would fail to notice the Japanese name. She had nothing left to cling to but a twisted sort of pride. Nor could she understand the GI by reading his expression. Offering only light and shadow, the photo pushed her away.

Outside, old tanks were lined up in a row, each tank designed to shut out the world save for the one element that faced out, a space popping up from the iron shell used to fire at people. Metal belts for legs created a perfect harmony between the two tasks of moving the tank forward and crushing everything in its path. Just being in the presence of these monsters, who forbade her from calling to them, who might have been machines or living things, was enough to make Kazuko shudder. She couldn't bring herself to look closely at the display. Even if she wanted to, it seemed her brain would harden and her senses turn to styrofoam. "Chotto, sumimasen," someone said from behind. Though the language was Japanese, the way the voice wavered on "sumi" sounded American. She turned to see a man in his mid-thirties with hair the yellow of a Japanese rose hanging down past his shoulders, and eyes the pale green of young bamboo. "Suddenly, I feel sick. I'm going to lie down here. Please wet this for me." He proceeded to lie down beside one of the tanks and close his eyes. Holding the towel he had handed her, Kazuko stood watching his body fold down like a collapsible chair until he was flat on his back. Something strange is going on here, she thought. Japanese-speaking Americans don't suddenly faint when a Japanese person is conveniently around to help them. Of course she didn't know whether he was actually American, not that it mattered anyway, and surely there would be no danger in dampening his towel. The moisture made the cloth so shapeless that even when she smoothed it out it wasn't square. Apparently the man hadn't lost consciousness, for he had both palms planted firmly on the ground. Kazuko folded the amorphous cloth and placed it on his forehead.

A stillness fell over the entire area. Kazuko moved away and knelt down to wait with her legs properly tucked under her. She didn't want to look at the tanks, so she gazed up at the sky. Not a single plane flew overhead. The man slowly pulled himself up. He sat in silence for so long she wondered if he had lost his Japanese until he finally came out with, "I don't feel so bad anymore. Thank you," leaving Kazuko with the impression that perhaps it was she who no longer felt sick. "James is my name," he said.

After the freedom of traveling on her own, the idea of joining up with another person seemed almost unbearable. When he suggested going to see a pagoda, the three Chinese characters used to write *stupa* flashed into her mind, but before she could follow the characters wherever they might take her, she had to decide what to do. "All right. Let's see the pagoda together. But after that I'm going on alone," she announced as she climbed into a cyclo. James hurriedly stepped up into a cyclo parked behind hers. When she saw the temple's name, Kaifuku-ji, Kazuko sat down on a bench and wrote, "His spine exploded overhead, the fragments bursting in midair. Lighter than dust, they crossed the sea. What happened to them after that, no one knows." The final "no one knows" was for atmosphere. Kazuko was fond of the wild little mutts stumbling around on wobbly legs, always playing around her, getting underfoot. Wherever she looked there were dogs. They neither howled at her, nor bounded over with wagging tails and eyes bright as shell buttons. They were simply small, and everywhere. Women were holding bunches of incense sticks in both hands like bouquets of long stemmed flowers, whipping them through the air, the fumes stinging her eyes and throat. Blinking furiously, she caught sight of James who seemed about to cry. Then whirling smoke enveloped her and the painful teardrops that bathed those green eyes faded from view. After a while the cloud thinned and gradually electric lights began to appear, *pika-pika chika-chika*, until she felt as if she were sitting in an arcade. The light bulbs seemed to be playing by a set of rules she didn't understand. Every other one went out, then every other two in triple time. Or so she thought until the whole thing changed. Diamonds, triangles, spinning around, look right, look left, then turning off. But this, too, was followed by an entirely different pattern. At the very center of all this illumination sat a statue of the Buddha. "This is like an arcade," Kazuko whispered to herself, though she was aware that someone who understood Japanese was now standing beside her. She hastily prayed that she wouldn't get pregnant. The main hall of the temple was so smoky she escaped into an alcove off to the side where she saw several Buddhas cradling babies. The infants were pieces of wood wrapped in red cloth tied with string, and six women in light summer dresses who all looked about twenty clasped their hands reverently before the altar. James had followed her but stopped short at the threshold. If these wooden slats swaddled in scarlet were what's born to Buddhas, then what about her parents who brought her into the world, and her grandparents and great-grandparents before them—what did they look like as new-borns? Kazuko wondered as she wandered dizzily back to the smoke-filled main hall. Seven papier-mâché figures with splendid beards appeared. Each was three times the size of a normal person and leaning slightly forward, staring down at her. Were these saints who had crossed the sea from China, or merchants? Whoever they were, once they arrived they must have copulated with great diligence to have produced so many descendents. Because Kazuko was a full-time tourist, she didn't want children. She possessed a passport that took the place of ancestors, and visas replaced offspring, but with no steady job her money always disappeared. Outside, she sat down on a bench and wrote in her notebook: "That night in her dream when the ship carrying her ancestors turned into smoked sardines." Then she said good-bye to James, who stood there with dried tears beneath his eyes and his hair in a tangle, and climbed into a cyclo.

The next day, Kazuko took a bus to the Cao Dai Temple in Tay Ninh. She felt like standing with someone in the shade of the fruit trees where they could press their sweaty bodies together, reaching up now and then to tickle each other's lips, wet with fruit juice, laughing all the while, so she regretted not having asked James the name of his hotel before they had parted. But being a tourist, she was obligated to go sightseeing every day. It was her duty to visit every famous place whether she wanted to or not, and under no circumstances was she permitted to criticize even the fake sites recently invented by travel agents. If a certain Ms. G considered meeting a boy whose skin she could touch to be the high point of a trip abroad, then Kazuko had a minor complaint for Ms. G. The task of the tourist was to express amazement and delight at scenery and cultural artifacts, and to pay for the privilege of seeing them. To go looking for love on top of that would be like eating a homemade lunch in a fancy restaurant. Dogs were everywhere here, too, sniffing around the bus stop. She could have watched the puppies play forever; boarding the bus now seemed like a terrible bore. She'd made up her mind to go, though, so she couldn't stop now. As the bus, packed with some thirty foreign tourists, rolled indecisively on and on along the edge where the city seemed to turn into village but never quite did, Kazuko looked out the window at primary- and middle- school children walking by and wanted to wave to them. A boy on his bicycle read a book as he steered with one hand. Its front wheel wobbling, the bicycle teetered down the narrow strip between cars and rice paddies. Without his book the boy might have peddled faster, but since time spent in between places is a part of life, too, reaching one's destination isn't necessarily the most important thing. If he swerved to the right, he would fall into a paddy field. But if he veered to the left, the bus carrying Kazuko and the other tourists would run him over.

A yellow church stood in the middle of what looked like a college campus. Perhaps "church" wasn't the right word for the Cao Dai Temple, but its rocket-shaped tower reminded Kazuko of one. What really bothered her about the church was its color—a yellow that weighed on her skin, mocked old age, and evoked neither comfort nor nostalgia. No sunflower or egg yolk hue. There was a category of people referred to as "yellow," though no color seemed more alien to Kazuko. And here it suddenly leaped out at her like a visitor from outer space. Not that she was frightened—she just didn't see how she could ever empathize with such a shade. Cao Dai, a mixture of Buddhism, Taoism, and Confucianism blended with the thought of Victor Hugo, was a religion with two million believers, most of whom lived in Vietnam, her guidebook said. Inside, rows of pillars towered over her. Something was wrapped around them, and because whatever it was looked friendly enough, she walked over for a closer look. Dragons, perhaps. That's certainly what they appeared to be from a distance. But up close she realized they couldn't be dragons because they didn't seem to have heads. Maybe the things started out as dragons made of ice cream and then were exposed to the yellow of the sun for so long that they melted, leaving only the remnants of their original shape. Bodies covered with red, white, and black scales mingled with swirling clouds and streamed down the yellow pillars like mud. Kazuko had stopped taking the pill since the day she left home. To see if the dragons had heads or not, she would have to circle around the pillars. However the worship service was underway on the first floor, forcing the tourists to retreat upstairs. She couldn't see the heads. These were not dragons. They were more like memories of dragons. On the second floor a group of girls stood in a corner singing a song that suggested the very image of *Central Asia*. The four girls frowned and threw the tourists occasional dirty looks. Tourists know what a nuisance they are, always barging into other people's lives. That's why Kazuko felt so uncomfortable no matter where she traveled, but as a tourist she simply had to endure the embarrassment until the end of the trip. Still, as no one had forced her to become a tourist, "endure" wasn't really the right word, though the fact that she had chosen this life didn't mean she could leave it behind whenever she pleased. Even if she wanted to, she couldn't quit in the middle of sightseeing. This looks like a Muslim mosque, she thought as she gazed down at the two hundred or so believers seated in ten rows on the floor below. The human figures looked like a part of the geometrical patterns embedded in the floor. The reds, blues, and yellows the believers wore could have been taken straight out of a mail-order catalog. Wondering what made this seem essentially different from a mosque, Kazuko realized that about two-thirds of the praying figures were female. Voices began to chant in a monotone that had no relation to the singing upstairs; on certain beats, the faithful simultaneously pressed their foreheads to the floor.

The huge windows that lined the walls should have let the sun stream in but didn't, at least not directly. Faint rays, like the light you see on a summer evening after wakening from too long an afternoon nap, gently bathed the interior. A large triangle was painted in the center of each window and an eye, complete with lashes, was painted within each triangle. Kazuko remembered the old man who ran her neighborhood electrical appliance store back in Japan, his eyes resembling the switches on the appliances he sold. Like a tourist with a standing-room ticket for the Viennese Opera, or for a single scene only at the Kabuki-za in the Ginza, Kazuko peered down at the service while snapping photos. A crowd of amateur photographers gathered around her. Cameras draw cameras. A Japanese man climbed the stairs, camcorder in hand. Japanese men have more stability with their shoes off than on. When German men pad down the wooden floor of an Asian corridor in white socks they look half dressed. A large head floated before her. So she was right about these creatures wrapped around the pillars after all. What a relief. These vaguely smiling dragons transported her back to childhood. Her reverie was broken by a voice behind her telling her what she already knew. "They're dragons." She turned around to see James standing there. He didn't crack a smile the day before, but today his mouth, rimmed with wisps of scraggly beard, was spread in a mocking grin. The hair on his face must have grown overnight. His red lips looked almost lewd. "So we meet again. Tourists collect in the same places," said Kazuko, to which James replied, "A community bound by fate," with an affected bow. His socks, once white, were now gray and the nail of his slightly protruding big toe peeked through a hole. Without putting on a show for the tourists, the believers continued to pray, their cloth-swathed backs revealing no sign of either pretentiousness or irritation. Cameras clicked on and off in turn, their flashes scattering down from the balcony. "We must be an awful bother to them," Kazuko murmured, meaning "we tourists." If these people were truly devout, outsiders would be a disturbance; if they welcomed spectators, didn't this mean their religion wasn't real? The confusion in Kazuko's mind could basically be broken down to such thoughts, but then a yellow dragon stuck its head in, waggling its cream-colored tongue, and devoured all her question marks. With her brain wrapped in an ambiguous yellow mist, Kazuko returned to the bus. James, too, retreated to his in silence.

She thought of the boy on his bicycle who read as he pedaled. On the way back, the bus stopped at the Cu Chi Tunnels, which were dug during the Vietnam War. A cut-away view was on display near the entrance to the museum. Work spaces, kitchens, and sleeping quarters were connect-ed by narrow corridors totaling some 200 kilometers in length. The man who provided this information didn't have scars on his cheeks but laughed as if he did. There was nothing caustic about his lightheartedness—no dark shadows or wounded sentiment. His smile exuded goodwill yet seemed to hide a store of anger within. "The reason why the passageways are so narrow in places was so the Americans, whose bodies are shaped differently from ours, wouldn't be able to crawl through," the man continued. There was a burst of laughter. He had lingered slowly over the phrase "bodies are shaped differently from ours" as if carefully searching for the right words. Kazuko thought of James, and looked for him in the crowd. As most tour buses bound for the Cao Dai Temple make a stop at the Cu Chi Tunnels, she figured he must be here somewhere. She spied several men with hair about the same color as his. The tunnel pursed its lips, warning people to keep out. The guide brushed away earth and fallen leaves to reveal a metal lid that looked like a manhole leading into the sewers, but the lid was barely the size of a large dictionary. While she was wondering how a human being could ever fit through, the cover suddenly opened and a soldier in a faded uniform stuck his head out and grinned. He nimbly slipped out and hopped to his feet. Applause crackled like a bonfire as a fireworks display of flashes and strobe lights brightened the air. Enveloped in a shadow the color of his fatigues, the soldier held the lid in one hand, his face wreathed in smiles. A young American placed one of his large Adidas sneakers over the entrance to the Cu Chi Tunnels, saying he might be

YOKO TAWADA

able to fit a leg in, maybe. Kazuko felt so stiff inside she couldn't even take her camera out of her bag. Though she didn't have any firsthand knowledge of World War II, she still couldn't imagine herself standing in front of an air raid shelter with a smile on her face, clutching a bamboo spear. Unlike Vietnam, Japan started a war of aggression, which left a residue of guilt; I'll never be able to look back on World War II proudly, with a sense of humor like these Vietnamese, she thought, feeling as though she alone had been snipped out of the picture with scissors and thrown into the wastebasket. The stinging deep within her eyes hurt so bad she couldn't keep them open. "This way seems a little too tight for you folks, so let's try the entrance for tourists, shall we?" the guide suggested, still beaming. Comparing the flesh on her belly and hips to the soldier's sinewy body, Kazuko realized she couldn't claim to look Vietnamese after all. The mouth of the Cu Chi Tunnels had been torn open and widened by force, the walls reinforced with cement to let tourists peek in. Yet the original earthen surface of these passageways was not for show, but to protect the people inside. Kazuko could initially walk bent over, but the tunnel quickly narrowed and before she knew it she was squatting, waddling like a duck. When her thigh muscles hurt too much she lowered onto all fours. The notion of inching along, her bottom thrust in the face of some unknown tourist behind gave her pause, but in a space that allowed no other way of moving, crawling soon seemed natural. Every so often openings dug into the ceiling let in light from above; crouching below she could peer through them at an angle and see the sky. Suppressing the need to escape, she crept forward. When the light disappeared, the darkness would worm its way deeper into her cheeks with every inch until she reached the next opening. Even if there was room enough to get through, with the sheer closeness pressing down on her spine as her field of vision closed like a wilting flower, where would her body go? Something inside her crumbled and she would soon unleash a wail as if possessed by some spirit. A force not her own was losing control, filling her yet utterly alien to her, making her want to scream. It was no use telling herself there was no danger, there was nothing to fear, for words like "fear" or "danger" existed in a different dimension. She was only aware the shriek about to escape from her lips. And once her voice was free of its cage, she might not be able to capture it again. A dampness that was neither the tunnel wall nor her own skin clung to her like a fishnet and she could no longer move. It was a frigid numbness, a sense of loathing about to explode; it was her mistrust of everything around her. This clammy web she was caught in could not be real; if she chanted a magic spell it would surely disappear. But nothing came to mind. Not even "dark." She was not trapped, she would eventually get out, she could go back as well as forward, she was not going to suffocate, she could not possibly die here. None of these reassurances had any effect.

And then, by a route as yet unknown to Kazuko, two words materialized: "all right." *ALL RIGHT.* The words were suddenly on her tongue then reached out to enshroud her shoulders and belly until her whole body was covered and the fishnet melted and disappeared. She climbed out of the tunnel, her blouse soaked with sweat and sticking to her skin. The muscles in her thighs ached. When American warplanes spied even a wisp of smoke from a cooking fire wafting up from the tunnel's mouth, they would attack, the guide explained. More bombs were used in Vietnam than in World War II. Back at her tour bus, Kazuko saw two other buses lined up waiting. James was leaning against one of them. His bangs were plastered to his pale, sweaty forehead, and his white clothes were so wet you could see the color of his skin. "Did you go in the Cu Chi Tunnels?" she asked. "I gave up at the entrance," he replied, without cracking a smile.

She couldn't forget the sight of the young boy steering his bicycle with one hand, an open book in the other. "Can you write all the letters in the Vietnamese alphabet?" If there was a certain Ms. G who insisted she had seen Ho Chi Minh on television asking a group of children this question, then Kazuko was Ms. G, and the sight of Vietnamese kids poring over their books brought tears to her eyes. Reading was a natural part of their lives. And they never doubted that the Roman alphabet was their own. The letters lined up on the pages might be the same as those used in the West, but the images these children spun from them were unique, beyond imitation. This wasn't simply a borrowed alphabet with a few extra flourishes—hair, perhaps, or horns—it was a complete metamorphosis. The letters were transformed like a dancer performing an entirely new dance. Ho Chi Minh saw his country's future strength not in mechanical engineering, capital, or underground resources, but in the literacy of the people, and so he was always asking the children, "Can you write your letters?" Ms. G would say, impassioned. The fact that a mere twelve percent of the Vietnamese population was illiterate made her so proud she felt a lump in her throat. Some mistakenly believed that a low GNP meant a high rate of illiteracy, ignoramuses subsequently sprouting up everywhere like bamboo shoots. "I hear over thirty-six percent of Americans can't read," Kazuko said, shooing away a fly with her left hand as she slowly lifted a glass of papaya juice to her lips with her right. The glass was lukewarm, and there were bubbles on the surface of the juice. "I am not American," James replied. They were in a makeshift teahouse, wooden tables and benches arranged on a dusty street corner. Face to face didn't feel right so they sat side by side, gazing at the road to avoid looking at each other.

The next morning, Kazuko found herself at a railway station that resembled the back of a storehouse. Three barefoot children spotted her and ran over, ropes in their hands. They mimed tying her bag up, nice and tight. Over to one side was a row of stalls. Each stall sold three different drinks, which were displayed in the same way in a line. She saw James standing with his back to her, a tall rucksack propped up beside him. From behind, his hair looked thinner than it did the day before, his hips as soft and round as a woman's. When Kazuko called, "Let's get going," he cringed as though he'd been scolded, then hesitantly turned around and smiled. "So you really came," he said with a surprised look, as if she hadn't agreed to go to Nha Trang with him. Perhaps it was unusual for tourists to keep their word. "Big Sis, promise on your finger."

Sucked in by the power of the passing trains, the tiny houses that lined both sides of the tracks seemed to be leaning inward. They looked close enough for you to reach through a window and grab a scrub brush from a kitchen. How long would it take them to get out of this alley? James left his seat and disappeared into the men's room just as a conductor in uniform entered the car to check tickets. In the seat ahead two plump, rosy-cheeked women in their mid-forties sat side by side, both wearing silk ao dai. When the conductor spoke to Kazuko in Vietnamese they clapped their hands over their mouths and giggled like high-school girls. They were probably thinking, She certainly isn't one of us. The conductor sneered and tried again, this time in English. "Ticket please." But what if a different person were sitting here at this very moment, her face identical to Kazuko's? The woman might indeed be Vietnamese, bound in eternal love to the American G.I. with whom she shared her life, Kazuko thought dreamily, and then James returned. Finding his faraway look rather pleasing, Kazuko gazed up at his profile and was about to speak when suddenly the skin around his eyes darkened, twitching violently for several seconds while his cheeks and lips loosened, his eyelids closed, and his neck dropped to one side causing his head to land squarely on her shoulder. Unsettled by the sudden weight but unable to say anything, Kazuko straightened her back and sat perfectly still, afraid that the slightest movement would send James's head crashing to the floor. Has he fainted? Kazuko asked herself, for there was no longer anyone else around to listen. Shouldn't I call a doctor? What if he just stays like this . . . ? she wondered, then closed her eyes, deciding not to worry. I'll go to sleep, too, that way they won't know who's ill and who's not. Maybe James was so exhausted that once a day his blood wandered down to the underworld. Perhaps fatigue drove certain tourists to travel in the first place. If she took slow, deep breaths, imagining waves breaking then flowing back to sea, counting them, taking care not to open her eyes, then she wouldn't have to think. But even behind her eyelids, the psychedelic aroma of food forced its way in and swirled through her body. The conductor was pushing a cart through the car, distributing meals in plastic containers like the in-flight meals on a plane. He handed her a box lunch of rice and boiled beans. The surface of the sticky rice was as smooth

YOKO TAWADA

as paper. She didn't know when James had removed his head from her shoulder and returned to his own seat. Steam rose from a huge kettle. The conductor poured soup with leafy greens into the cup embedded in her plastic tray. The soup tasted of shellfish. "So you're with us again," Kazuko said in the casual tone she would have used with a roommate who had awaken from an afternoon nap. The greens swimming so elegantly in the hot broth died crisply between her teeth. Squinting into the sunlight, James blinked several times and appeared to be smiling. He picked up each bean one by one as if he had used chopsticks his entire life. "How come you speak Japanese?" The words were out before she could stop them. She had more interesting questions in mind for him, but out of fear or just plain laziness, this is the one she ended up asking. "Because I'm Japanese," he answered gravely. "And how did that happen?" she countered, a bit put out, but James, sipping his shellfish soup, calmly threw the query back at her. "What about you? How did you become Japanese?"

If you cut off ears of rice and throw them away, would you get an earache? And why shouldn't bread have ears, too? People say dizzy spells are caused by a breakdown in the balancing mechanism deep within the inner ear. The Japanese are prejudiced against foreign rice, so why don't they complain about foreign bread? The train raced through open fields, leaving the alley far behind. Rather than towering majestically, the mountains humbly bowed. The ground was so wet you couldn't tell whether it was land or water. Kazuko replied, "As the train sank into the swamp, blue sky welled up from beneath her feet."

Kazuko and James pressed their ears together, listening. "This is an ear-kiss," James said. When his jaw moved, bristles of beard he had missed shaving scratched the tender skin below Kazuko's earlobe. They sat caressing each other's kneecaps, moving their fingers around and around. An electric current ran from their knees through their thighs to deep within their bladders. At 10 p.m. the train finally arrived at Nha Trang. They walked out of the station leaning against each other to find twenty cyclos waiting. It was so troubling trying to decide whether to stay in the same room with James that Kazuko started chanting the name of a hotel from her guidebook like a mantra that would show her a way out of this dilemma. Two cyclo drivers took off like kidnappers with Kazuko and James. Was she sure *that* hotel was the one she wanted? the driver asked pointedly, puzzling Kazuko. Tourists never know their true desires. Did she *really* want to go there, was that *really* what she wanted to do? Kazuko silently egged her cyclo on, "Faster, faster," as it raced along the shore. Not that she was in a hurry; the Pacific Ocean was blacker than the night. She turned around several times to see if James's cyclo was following behind. Each time she turned, he lifted a hand toward his chest while sitting like a Buddhist statue, his palm shining white in the light of the street lamps. When the cyclos finally stopped under a mountain of darkness, the shadowy skeleton of a five-story building loomed before them. Long ago a conch shell the size of a dinosaur washed onto the shore. The shell's still there, only now it's called a construction site. The hotel's name, at least, was clearly written on a sign that resembled a cornerstone. They must be rebuilding the hotel, she thought, but here in the middle of the night with no one around, it was hard to imagine these metallic bones ever taking on flesh again. The sound of the waves bathed the portals of her ears. The cyclo drivers were gone, and James's face was growing pale. This was where she had told them to bring her, so she couldn't really complain. James twisted around to get closer to the steel skeleton, then plunked down on the ground. "Looks like this hotel is where we're going to stay," sighed Kazuko. Because the empty shell didn't have walls or floors or ceilings, there were no rooms, and thus she needn't worry about the sleeping arrangements. James was leaning against a pillar with his eyes closed, sweat beading out on his forehead. "Please wet a towel for me," he said, and this time Kazuko rushed to retrieve one from his rucksack and searched in vain for a pipe or spigot, anything that might yield water. "Please wet a towel for me" is a set phrase he's reserved for me, she thought, forcing her shaky legs to carry her down to the beach. In the darkness something rose up from the bottom of the sea and thrust out its horns only to fall headfirst, shattering into the sand. She wasn't able to tell how close she could get to the water and still be safe. Figuring that the ocean would start where the darkness was deepest, she stood still, straining to see, feeling patches of chilly air. The night looked diaphanous in some places and muddy in others, though nothing revealed where the water began. This is the PACIFIC OCEAN, she thought, and the moment the name flashed into her mind, she saw the sea. Running over as if to pounce on it, she squatted down and dipped the towel in. An instant later the low roar she heard turned into an avalanche that assaulted her, drenching her hips, stomach, and chest with a load of salt water. Gasping for breath she managed to escape to higher ground, but sensing neither the humiliation that would make her want to weep nor the wellspring from which tears might come, she returned to the construction site. James had fallen over onto his side, his hips and knees at perfect right angles. The weight of the towel, cold and slightly sticky, covered his pulsating forehead. Kazuko peeled off her wet clothes and hung them on the scaffolding to dry. It was a warm, windless night. After she changed into dry clothes, she lay down with her back pressed up against James's and closed her eyes. Staring hard into the unfamiliar darkness had made her eyes heavy.

James's body rolled as the earth rotated so when the sun rose beyond the sea, he was sleeping with his chest pressed against Kazuko's back. They awoke at nearly the same time to the rumbling of trucks and scattered laughter from pass-

YOKO TAWADA

ing bicycles, and after hurriedly getting their things to-gether, headed for the main street. James's lips were cherry red again, and the towel, still damp, smelled faintly moldy. They didn't walk far before they found a pension where a man with a face like a child wearing spectacles with metal frames informed them that rooms were available. He also told them where they could find a doctor, and they set off immediately. Although employed by the state-run hospital, the doctor examined patients at his home when he was free in the evenings, and on weekends and holidays, for a slightly higher fee. Many doctors kept the same work schedule, but this doctor had an especially good reputation, the man at the pension explained with a smile. The doctor repeated his stock diagnoses and symptoms, varying them slightly as he examined James. James caught a cold, he had been working too hard, he wasn't getting proper nourishment. His nasal membranes were slightly swollen, his eyes were a little red, the surface of his tongue was rough, his voice was hoarse, his skin was dry and scaly, and was his urine perhaps darker than usual? Did he have diarrhea? Nausea? James looked healthy enough now, but in fifteen minutes he might turn pale and faint again, Kazuko thought without saying any-thing. For all she knew, James was inhaling pockets of deadly gas that were waiting for him, lurking in the air, the poison spreading through his entire system. "Can you do a test for AIDS here?" he asked out of the blue, causing the doctor to freeze for several seconds before replying, "Of course," in a casual tone as he took some black-and-white pamphlets from a drawer. "I'd like to be tested, too," said Kazuko, as though she were completely removed from the situation.

She never imagined she'd be getting an AIDS test in Vietnam. And she certainly didn't expect to stay this long in Nha Trang, a town she hadn't even heard of before. James seemed to be feeling better. He didn't know the results yet, but at least the test was over, or maybe the fish god of the Po Nagar Cham Tower cheered him up. When they first saw it they both burst out laughing like a windstorm whipping sand from a dune. The fish god was the strangest-looking stone figure ever, with the plum-shaped eyes of an Asuka Buddha, the features of a sea bream, a mammoth's ears, and what appeared to be a ski cap on its head. The ears gave it a mousy look. Wavy grooves crossed its cheeks. It sat in the lotus position, a winsome pout on its face. "Let's start a new religion, just the two of us—this can be our god," said Kazuko, clasping her hands in prayer, but then turned to find James frowning. "I can't. I'm a Christian." Upset by the hardness of his words, Kazuko rushed out of the tower in silence. An old woman, bent with age, was sweeping the grounds with a tiny broom. A white cat perched atop a broken brick followed her every move with swollen eyes. The cat departed when James emerged from the tower. "What makes you claim to be Japanese, or Christian?" asked Kazuko, still out of breath. "Once something's been destroyed it can never be restored. Champa culture will never come back," James replied. "You mean it's beyond all hope? I'm not so sure about that." Perhaps because she was a tourist, Kazuko found his pessimism unconvincing. The Pacific Ocean crashed on the shore at the feet of tourists, but the waves always returned to their original form. "Seems I came all the way to Vietnam only to get sick. Even as a kid I was a weakling, my head ached all the time, and I've never been to war." Two puppies at play came rolling out of a bamboo hut onto the beach. "There're a lot of ruined buildings in Vietnam, but can't they be rebuilt? I don't believe that what's been broken can't be put back together." "But what about Champa? Champa will never return."

Grilled on skewers, sausages as long as ring fingers tasted like the meat of several unknown species mashed together. They were wrapped in rice paper with raw bean sprouts and greens, and then dipped in a peanut sauce. The translucent rice paper film, shaped like a leaf, transformed the curly tops of the sprouts into mere shadows, giving the whole roll an almost abstract appearance. "Aren't you going to eat it?" "How can I when I don't know what it is?" "Are you trying to tell me you always know exactly what's in your food? Haven't you ever eaten a hamburger at a fast food restaurant?" "I'm not American, so I never eat that stuff." Kazuko sprinkled enough chili pepper on hers to numb her tongue. As it scorched her mouth, the red-hot spice burned away the cloud of mist in her mind. Though they were supposed to be laughing, celebrating their health, James didn't even chuckle. "That meat might be your fish god. Still want to eat it?" "Sure. I'd consider myself blessed. You eat bread and say it's the body of Christ, don't you?" An embarrassed smile twitched around James's lips. Then, his eyes shining with a silver light, he said, "Let's go back to the hotel. Right now," and swallowed hard. This worried Kazuko a little.

Still standing, they embraced, but when James slipped his fingers inside her underwear and boldly started playing the piano on her bottom, Kazuko felt she had to say something. "I have a friend in Hué. I promised her I'd visit." His lips and hands swelled way out of proportion, and he licked her body like a monstrous octopus. The ten digits that found such pleasure in the firm flesh of her hips now discovered openings in the rear, first one then another, and eagerly sought entrance. Twisting and turning, Kazuko wondered in horror why her body was so full of holes. Five, six, seven, ecstasy flowed through all her tubes. Eight, nine, ten. Finally the single word "Why?" seeped out of her. She no longer knew where her body ended; it had transformed into wrinkles of air that seemed to fan out forever. If this quivering continued she would lose any semblance of form and everything would spill out, she thought, then desperately widening her eyes, she pushed James away. The fish god slept on.

Arrival in Da Nang brought her one step closer to Hué. Not that she was in a hurry to get there. But knowing that

if she let her travel fever carry her off in a thousand different directions she would never reach her destination,
Kazuko forced herself to focus on the road to Hué, which
was also the road to Hanoi, leading ultimately to the
Chinese border. "This must be a war remnant they haven't
gotten around to filling in yet." The pit in front of the station was big enough for a person to squat down in. People
turned away from this open wound as they passed by. James
glared at Kazuko, his eyes full of hate. Pained to the heart
by this man who spat pus at her with no explanation,
Kazuko responded by repeating the question, "How come
you speak Japanese?" What she had intended to ask was
why, though he could speak her language, he had nothing
meaningful to say to her, but in her confusion this was all
she could manage. "Because I'm Japanese. As I told you
before. Time and again." "What about your parents, then—
what nationality were they?" A thorn appeared between his
eyes. "I don't have any. They supported the Vietnam War, so
I cut them off." James walked on in silence. Once they were
inside their hotel room, he abruptly grabbed Kazuko by the
elbow and shook her, screaming, "You don't suffer at all!
You don't even think!" Sobbing, she answered, "That's only
natural . . . I'm a tourist . . . it's my duty not to think."
Scientific analysis reveals that tears of anguish have the
same chemical composition as those shed while chopping
an onion. Kazuko ran out of the hotel and slowed to a
walk, hoping to find a crowd to lose herself in. It was get-

ting dark. She was searching for something here in Da Nang, but not knowing exactly what, she decided to look for the Cao Dai Temple. She glanced to the left and right and saw herself strolling along on each side, wearing her face as if this were perfectly normal. Behind her she saw another one. "Hey there! Where're you headed?" "To the Cao Dai Temple." "Really? Imagine that . . ." She neared the soccer stadium. The wall around the stadium stretched so far she began to lose her sense of purpose. Where was she headed when she left the hotel? Perhaps the heat was causing a dullness in her chest, making her anxious to reach some destination, no matter where. The tiny lights on the plastic Christmas trees grew brighter. Surrounded by more and more faces and backs, she was having trouble keeping track of the different Kazukos around her. She'd be better off without these equivocal copies, but she was terribly worried that if all of her selves were to become hopelessly lost she would have no idea who would remain. Mountains of Chinese herbal medicine, toilet paper, and soap towered in the shops. Tea bags and leather belts and flyswatters hung from ceilings. Countless faces, buying and selling. Bits of trash between the rusty railroad tracks, trash that turned into vegetables and seashells as she walked with her head down. Women had spread their wares on straw mats by the side of the road, and when Kazuko slipped around the mats to avoid stepping on all their vegetables and seashells, a girl with a pole slung over her shoulder loomed before her while

YOKO TAWADA

a bicycle screeched to a halt from behind. Baskets of raw eggs and fish were thrust in her face. Wondrous patterns on quail eggs and saggy white blocks of tofu whispered in her ear, "Buy me, buy me." To reach her destination she needed to get through the market. But where was she going exactly? There was no place she wanted to go. Nor could she turn back. If only she could collapse right here and go to sleep with a blanket over her head to block out all the sights.

As she finally accepted that there was no place to sit in the market, Kazuko saw a sign for a state-run hotel. "State-run" meant one needn't buy anything, so in effect it was a rest house. A sleepy-looking youth in a suit stood at the reception desk; to her query, "Restaurant?" he glumly replied, "Second floor." The deserted lobby furnished with red vinyl sofas reminded her of a Russian hotel during the Soviet era. Here she could relax. No one would coax her to buy eggs or ride in a cyclo. The twenty or so tables in the restaurant looked like a holiday parade. Teacups and chopsticks were placed neatly around each table, and one lonely looking waitress stood in a corner. A state-run hotel can be compared to a temple perched on a mountaintop, its back turned on the secular world. As if she were wounded, Kazuko fell into a chair. The menus were printed in both Chinese and Russian. She took out her notebook. "I want to tear this tablecloth into bandages to wrap around my face." She finished writing and looked up to discover not the waitress but James standing over her. His eyes were red and swollen, his voice husky. Hearing him whine, "I can't stay in Vietnam alone," Kazuko hung her head. "I died here in the war, more than twenty years ago." "Stop talking and sit down." When Kazuko ordered two coffees the waitress gave her rather than James a strange look. They sat perfectly still until their coffees arrived. Vietnamese coffee is the color of ink, and when the condensed milk that collects in the bottom is stirred with a tiny aluminum spoon, its sticky sweetness swirls up like a fluffy summer cloud. Kazuko pinched the back of James's hand twice. "We're tourists, so we mustn't cry. Tourists don't have emotions."

On the way back to their room it started to rain, so they bought a pair of pink plastic raincoats for a dollar, the vinyl so thin their clothes showed through underneath. Nevertheless, they looked like fraternal twins, two bodies side by side wrapped in the same pale membrane. Raindrops dripped loudly from their coats onto the floor as they stood in their hotel room groping each other without being able to touch flesh. Feeling James's impatience in the rustling of the plastic, Kazuko's lower abdomen grew hot. The moment she touched the plastic over his crotch, someone next door must have turned a radio on, for the rhythm of a popular song filled the room. "The man I used to be took a part of me with him when he died. Now I'm only a locust's shell. But my soul can enter the body of a woman," said James, and feeling something the size of a fist start to pulsate in her vagina, Kazuko let out a cry. "You won't believe me, but it's true." Pressing down hard with both hands on the quivering mass within her belly, Kazuko finally managed to blurt out, "You mustn't give your soul to another person." But James's soul gushed out, soaked in thick bodily fluid. "Let's go to Hué tomorrow by bus." "I can go back inside you whenever I please." "We'll be crossing Hai Van Pass, you know." Kazuko tore off her raincoat and clothing and jumped into the shower. The cold water clawed at her skin, instantly drawing the nerves to the surface. The nerve endings then trembled and turned into drops that rolled off her body.

There was something terribly nostalgic about the name Hai Van Pass. Lulled by exhaust fumes and the lethargic swaying of the bus, Kazuko thought that perhaps she had been born in a house near the pass, which would explain why the name sounded so familiar. Maybe she had only been there that one time and then it vanished from her memory. People can forget their own name if they live long enough without using it. Under the tires of the bus was a mountain road, below which spread a valley, its wide-open mouth filled with mist. "So now I've finally come home," Kazuko announced in a voice loud enough for everyone to hear. The woman in front of her turned around and scolded, "You're Japanese and you know it. So just keep quiet." Kazuko was about to fire back, "And what are you, then?" when she gasped in shock, for she was looking into her own face. "We're crossing Hai Van dorsal fin / Rain flowers fall around us," sang a voice from the seat behind. Kazuko looked back to see a brand-new acoustic guitar, shiny with a yellow varnish the same shade as the Cao Dai Temple. "That's my guitar you're playing," Kazuko said, and was nearly on her feet when the bus lurched violently forward, throwing her back down. The teenage girl strumming chords was also Kazuko. "That's precisely what I was talking about," said a husky voice. It was the Kazuko in front, talking to yet another Kazuko ahead of her. "The real tourists are the ones who think they're the only ones who aren't tourists." Peering into the mirror at the faces of his female passengers, the driver said, "If you'd like we can make an eight-minute stop here. Would anyone like to take a picture of Hai Van Pass?" Mist shrouded the entire view; a photograph would be pointless. Kazuko wanted to leave her camera in her lap and go to sleep. She wasn't in the mood for snapping photos. But if she said she didn't care to stop, the driver, obviously proud of Hai Van Pass, would be terribly disappointed. Kazuko started complaining again. "Believing you can understand how someone else feels is sheer arrogance. You're assuming that other people see the world within the limits of your own imagination. That's why you . . ." Kazuko interrupted her, blurting out, "I can't see anything, so you needn't stop for me." It was a courageous statement. Rather than making polite excuses like, "I'm sure everyone's in a hurry," or, "It's a shame the weather's so bad," she honestly admitted that she couldn't see Hai Van Pass. Her voice, reverberating deep within her, was strong enough to open cracks in her skin. Her right shoulder was being smooshed and warmed by the heat of James's head, while the rest of her seemed about to shatter and fly into the air. James was sound asleep. His body was still wrapped in a layer of pink plastic as was Kazuko's. The flimsy material was already torn in two places under the arms. James murmured something in a language Kazuko couldn't understand. "When we get to Hué," the driver exclaimed cheerfully, "I'll stop the bus in front of Trang Tien Bridge." James mumbled something again. "When we get to Hué," said Kazuko. "I told you so," Kazuko replied. "You've got it all wrong," retorted Kazuko.

SAINT GEORGE AND THE TRANSLATOR

. . . in, approximately, ninety percent, of the victims, almost all, always, on the ground, lying, shown as, desperately raising, heads, on display, are, attack weapons, or, the points of, in their throats, stuck, or . . .

Gripping my fountain pen as if it were a knife I looked out the window. Dark cacti protruded sporadically from the sandy slope stretching out before me for a distance that might have been far or near I couldn't tell which before being swallowed up by ominous waves of banana trees with the sea beyond although there was no visible boundary to show where water turned into sky. The sea doesn't ascend and gradually become sky nor are sea and sky like two countries that meet at the border; in fact they exist entirely independently of each other so it's odd to regard them as two colors side by side as if looking at a landscape painting. It seems wherever you go the scenery appears exactly like a picture and I hate that. Furthermore as I didn't come to the Canary Islands for sightseeing it was embarrassing to look out the window and find myself gazing at the ocean like a tourist.

On the sea's purple surface I could see stripes that I assumed were waves though they seemed to be stuck or frozen. So perhaps they weren't waves at all and something entirely different caused this striped pattern to appear on the water. Besides the sea could be farther away than I thought. Seen from a distance moving objects do sometimes seem to be standing still. The moon for instance is in constant motion but you wouldn't know just by glancing up. Upon further consideration there was actually nothing surprising about stationary waves. I couldn't hear them either for that matter nor could I smell the rank odor of seaweed or dead fish so the sea must have been far away after all. My friend wasn't lying when she described this place as "a house with an ocean view"; it was just that the "view" was from a distance. But this didn't bother me in the least. I hate to swim anyway so it didn't matter if the sea was near or far and in fact the further away it was the less I had to worry about it which suited me perfectly.

Though the ocean was static I could see the heavy leaves on the banana trees in front of it stir in unison every time the wind picked up even though the banana grove was also quite a distance away. I was there only yesterday which made the grove seem close but when I remembered how far I walked I could hardly call it near.

The moment I thought of the banana grove my right arm started to itch. Especially around the wrist and elbow it stung like vinegar so I stuck my arm out the window into the light but as usual all I saw were skin pores. Bright sunlight sometimes makes me itchy. Usually I hardly notice but when I remembered those banana trees the itchiness got so bad I could barely stand it. Or at least I thought it was getting worse. Wondering if I was imagining things I put my arm into the light again and while I was examining the pores the itchiness intensified. So it seemed I wasn't hallucinating after all. But these days allergies of this kind are far from uncommon and in fact I don't think I've ever met a woman who's never had problems with her skin. I decided there was nothing to worry about. Fishing an old towel that smelled slightly of cement from the cupboard I wet it at the sink and wrapped it around my right arm. Everything you needed was here in the house but I didn't know who had last used the towels or why. My friend's brother was an internist who had bought this place as a "summer villa" a decade or more ago though he hardly had any time to come here himself and has generously let friends and relatives use it. When he said he preferred to stay at home and imagine other people staying here I thought at first it was sour grapes but he took me out to dinner several times and after we talked I began to believe he might be telling the truth. Twice he suggested that I come too but I refused both times. Whenever I don't want to do something I never hesitate to say so and often end up feeling guilty later. My main reason for rejecting his offer was that I found the thought of being on the island and the doctor imagining me here the whole time somehow embarrassing. There were lots of other reasons I couldn't explain myself. Yet the third time he asked I suddenly felt I absolutely had to go. "It's best to go with someone," he said but I came by myself. "Not even a man should go alone but a woman definitely needs a traveling companion," the doctor told me over the phone. "I'll be fine. After all I'm not a tourist," I answered and here I was all by myself.

The towel was cold and heavy at first but the warmth of my arm soon penetrated the chill turning the towel luke-warm before quickly drying it out. When I tried to slowly bend my arm the towel was as hard as a cast and wouldn't bend. Using my left hand I placed the fountain pen into my right and pretended to be wounded.

. . . in open mouths, in throats, stuck, stabbed, tongue at the bottom, run through . . .

Tomorrow morning Wednesday the day foreign planes and ships arrive George might come to the island looking for me. If he were to come at all it would be tomorrow. Just thinking about it made me nervous. If I didn't finish today there'd be no working with him here and I wouldn't make the deadline. Ever since I landed on this island I've thought of nothing else but translating this "story" and now with only one day left I still didn't know how to do it. I wasn't even sure whether these clusters of roman letters covering a mere two pages could even be called a "story." Fiction should feel like a borrowed coat softened by many wearings but these groups of letters were like grains of sun-baked sand that won't stick to your skin so you couldn't start reading them as if you were slipping your arms through the sleeves of a coat. Reading this "story" was like walking around wearing sand rather than a coat.

The word for "victims" began with an "O." I noticed there were "O's" scattered across the first page. Or perhaps it would be better to say that the page was full of holes eaten away by the letter "O." There was a wall behind formed by the white page so I couldn't see inside and the harder I looked the more it seemed I'd never break through. I colored the insides of all the "O's" black with my fountain pen and felt a slight sense of relief.

I didn't know the banana grove was built like a prison until the day before. Initially I couldn't figure out what I was looking at—gray concrete blocks stacked up and secured by barbed wire. The blocks formed a wall about two meters high that continued on and on along the road and because there wasn't a break no matter how far I walked I finally couldn't keep myself from pressing my nose to a crack and peering in to see banana trees lined up in rows and planted exactly the same distance apart. Bunches of bananas were covered with blue semitransparent plastic bags tightly tied with rope at the bottom. The bags were clouded with steam inside and through the plastic you could see droplets trickling down. What surprised me was that the earth the trees grew out of was flat and bald without a single blade of grass. Also missing were the sounds of living things so the whole area was absolutely silent. There were no birds or bees or dogs. A little further on there was a tin door in the wall that seemed too small to walk through without bending over. The door was misshapen and looked as if it might pop open at any moment so I pushed it but it was locked. Beside the door was a sign made of plywood. Painted on the sign in white was the picture of a skull. The message below announced in crude handwriting that entry was forbidden because the air inside was poisonous. The thought of the compound having been sprayed with a pesticide so strong it would instantly turn you into a skeleton made me even more eager to sneak in. Turning around I caught sight of a man in a straw hat. Looking down I took off my shoe in order to shake out the gravel and hoped he wouldn't notice me.

. . . ninety percent, of the victims, mouths, sewed shut . . .

The word I translated as "mouth" was used only for the mouths of animals never humans. I drew two lines through the word "victim" and wrote "sacrifice" instead. Sacrifice. A sacrifice needn't be human. The mouths of sacrifices. My new choice didn't sound right either. I rubbed my ring finger across my upper lip from left to right and discovered a little bump like an insect bite just right of center. When I touched the bump I felt a sharp pain and then an unbearable itchiness. It couldn't be a mosquito bite. I remembered the internist confidently telling me there were no mosquitoes on the island. This felt like the tingling you feel in your lip when the tiny transparent hairs hidden on the seemingly smooth skin of a peach you start sucking on not really out of hunger but just for fun pierce the skin and infuse your lips with acidic juices. I wanted to tear my upper lip from my mouth. Then I thought of putting it in an empty imported tea can as a present for George.

. . . and, almost all, always, they, alone, are, friends, people to help them, relatives, near, are not . . .

The house where I was staying alone was of a simple construction: the weird pieces of rock that rolled down during a volcanic eruption had been piled up and cemented in place which seemed "simple" to me although I could be mistaken since I've never built a house and yet these stones of many different sizes certainly appeared to have been arranged in a haphazard manner. Perhaps it was the work of an amateur who had let the pieces fall where they may. But then why would those two small round stones have been placed like stars above the diagonal of that huge diamond-shaped slab? I wondered and as I carefully examined each section I decided the pattern couldn't possibly have been due to chance. You couldn't fit rocks together in this way without thinking which meant that whoever had done it must have had something in mind. But what? I had no idea. What people think about while they're assembling rocks is completely beyond me.

Hardened lava flowed by the house and continued in a narrow belt down to the sea. The black path was like a "river." I didn't know what else to call it. At dusk the path looked like a real "river" and I could even hear the sound of water. I found myself walking on that black river beside a woman I had never seen before. Without asking I knew she was the "author." As she walked the author sometimes stumbled and almost fell but in such a charming way that without thinking I almost reached out to help her although I couldn't tell whether she had really lost her footing or was just pretending. She was twenty years older than me so it seemed unfair that her clumsiness could be so winsome but then again women of her generation must have had to be attractive in order to make a living I thought deciding to accept this rationale for the time being. It wasn't the author's charm itself that made me jealous so much as the fact that it existed for the benefit of an indefinite number of men I didn't know.

The burnt charcoal-like substance under our feet would occasionally crack with a dry popping sound. Through the holes left behind we could see dark caves of immeasurable depth spread out beneath us making me wonder what would happen if we fell. But as I'd hate to hear the author say "You're as timid as a deer" I pretended I wasn't afraid. Nothing frightened me more than clichéd criticism. Yet when I was with someone who didn't seem likely to deliver one hackneyed saying after another for some reason I myself could think of nothing but trite phrases. When I picked up a broken piece of lava it was as light as styrofoam and colored my fingers black which clearly outlined my fingerprints clearly.

"Does it look like there's a cut on my face?" asked the author. Cautiously I looked up at her. I saw nothing like a "cut" not even a "face" just a blank space shaped like the letter "O".

. . . *completely, seldom, most, from the background, emerge, one or two, young ones, appear, at times, stay of execution, is granted, murderous, sight, wounds of the heart, however, cannot be avoided, for that very reason, they also, as though they're trying to howl, look, at any rate, their, small mouths, wide, are open . . .*

What kind of suckling beasts would open their mouths so wide? They might be something like cicada larvae or perhaps baby birds. Whatever they were I had a warm almost nostalgic feeling toward them although I couldn't remember the sound of those howling voices. Somehow I seemed to be thirsty again. The air here was so dry your throat was always parched even if you didn't move. The island itself seemed desiccated. I remembered the doctor explaining to me how the banana trees needed so much moisture that subterranean water had to be continually pumped up to spray them so the soil was left completely dry. Nevertheless the view that it would be unfeasible to stop exporting bananas both from a diplomatic and an economical stand-point was accepted as established fact. The doctor himself seemed convinced of this but to me such an argument was like saying people in so-called developing countries would immediately starve to death if economic aid were cut off which I also didn't believe. I put my lips to the earthenware pot in the corner of the kitchen and drank. The handle either because it was poorly made or perhaps due to mold felt rough and hurt my palm. I didn't have any gloves though so I had to pick things up barehanded.

While I was squatting by the entrance to the banana grove shaking the gravel out of my shoe the man in the straw hat spoke to me.

"Did you come for this? Or this?" he asked first mimicking the breaststroke and then mountain climbing.

"Neither. I came here to translate."

"Oh, I see."

Contrary to my expectations he didn't look the least bit surprised which embarrassed me and I regretted even having brought up the subject rather than simply saying work.

Now he was standing there in silence and it was my turn to speak. "I'm translating a story from a foreign language into my own," I added uselessly.

I wished I hadn't said that either but it was already too late. When I have nothing to say I tend to pointlessly talk too much.

Leaning against the concrete wall the man suddenly said, "Think you'll make it in time?" He touched a nerve which startled me at first but I told myself he must be either shooting in the dark or talking about something entirely unrelated to what was worrying me.

"I have to finish in time. There's money involved you know," I lied. Even if I did finish I probably wouldn't get paid and furthermore the magazine specializing in literature in translation where I was planning to publish the piece had been in the red so long my friends were afraid it would fold before anyone received royalties for the next issue. So I'd have to compensate for the loss by working random jobs to earn my living expenses though the reason I absolutely had to get this translation done on time was an entirely different matter. I had made a habit of mentioning money because it always seemed to help the conversation flow smoothly even with people I didn't know.

The man stood and stared as if he didn't hear me which made me so mad I wanted to slap him with a really nasty remark. I prepared one in the back of my throat: If money means nothing to you then why are you working in this banana grove? But I kept silent and I was happy that I did. After all a man wearing a straw hat standing next to a banana grove doesn't necessarily work there; this man merely fit my image of what a fruit picker might look like. I actually knew nothing about men whose work involved physical labor. So it was rude of me to try to read his thoughts and perfectly natural perhaps that I didn't have a clue as to what was going through the mind of a person of the opposite sex in a straw hat whom I wasn't even sure was a laborer in the first place.

. . . for them, is waiting, the same, lot, they, grow up, into it, to become sacrifices, just once, far from that, are shown, the young, together, being killed, with one stroke, two at a time . . .

Unconnected words scattered across the page. I knew I had to link them together into sentences but I was physically deficient. My lung capacity wasn't good enough. "The trick is to read one sentence slowly while taking a deep breath, hold your breath while you translate the sentence in your head and rearrange the words, then, while carefully exhaling, write the translation down," my translator friend Ei told me but reading only one word left me panting and with all these breathless thoughts running through my head I couldn't seem to get to the next one. Even so I was at least being faithful to the unfamiliar texture of each word and I was beginning to think maybe this was more important for the time being. At least I created the sensation of throwing each word over to the other side with great care. Which was why the entire text was breaking into fragments but I simply didn't have the energy to think about the whole. The whole didn't even seem to matter. If translation meant "passing something over to the other side" then perhaps forgetting about the "whole" and starting out with fragments wasn't a bad idea. But then again translation might be something entirely different. Perhaps translation was something like metamorphosis. Both the words and the story were transformed into something entirely new. Then all the words should casually line up on the page as if they had always looked this way. I could never pull this off which must mean I was a lousy translator. At times the thought that I myself might turn into something else before the words did was absolutely terrifying.

University professors occasionally criticize my work. Other translators haven't though scholars seem to think translators are like students and like to point out my mistakes and dismiss my style as "translationese" while complaining that my Japanese is wrong or my use of Chinese characters strange. One scholar even wrote in a review, "Due to the blatant 'translationese' one simply cannot feel one is reading a literary work." As there's no money in translating literature and certainly little praise my friend Ei gave it up altogether and started to write novels. Although Ei has suggested I do the same and I've gotten similar advice from others as well I keep translating despite having to work random jobs which gives people the impression that I'm overly confident in my ability when actually I'm not. How could I be when I've never received a single word of encouragement from anyone? Once an author I translated did get a few favorable comments but even then the reviewers moaned "If only it weren't for the terrible 'translationese' style" or "It's a shame we can't experience the flavor of the original" which means that far from praising my work they were actually blaming me for everything they didn't like.

For me one unpleasant thought invariably leads to an endless string of anxieties. And now there was plenty to worry about: Not just whether I'd finish but when I was ready to go home would I be able to find a plane ticket right away and if so could I pay for it and if not who would I borrow the money from and what to do about the key to the basement I had lost? That lost key haunted me while I was translating. And furthermore the hand that held the fountain pen itched so bad I was forced to stop writing after every line to put the pen down and scratch my palm.

. . . especially, have met, people, the sacrifices, in churches, in chapels, in

*monasteries, in art museums, they, as before said, alone, however, not
entirely, accompanied, by their torturers . . .*

I had an intriguing encounter in the island church with
something I had once seen in the National Gallery in
London. It happened two days ago while I was on my way
to the market to buy some bread and cheese. Since the slope
to the village was terraced I couldn't see the grocery or the
church from my window but when I walked down I realized
for the first time how many places were hidden from view.
In one such place I found the church—a conglomeration of
black stones. The use of black stones in buildings was now
prohibited so this structure stood out as a particularly
impressive one though I couldn't understand why the
islanders who thought black was the devil's color would
have chosen this stone for their church. Roman Catholics
had occupied the island some five hundred years ago the
doctor said and for some reason this date alone stuck out
clearly in my mind while I had forgotten the many others
such as the years of the volcanic eruptions which seemed
like a terrible loss now. The doctor often talked in statistics.
So often in fact that I couldn't remember any of them. He
knew exactly how many tourists visited each year and the
number of plant species that grew only on this island and
even the annual production of bananas in tons but these
numbers were completely erased from my memory.

The entire church was leaning forward. Maybe this is why I pushed the door open and walked straight in as if I were being pulled by a magnet. The air inside was cold and dank. Dim rays shone from a small lattice window onto a picture someone had hung between two stone pillars as if to hide it but the light was too weak for me to clearly see what was there—alive. The dark colors in the center seemed to drink in the feeble glow. Frustrated I stood motionless before the picture. As my eyes adjusted to the dark I glimpsed something round and blood-soaked with a spear sticking out of it which I thought must be the "eye" of a living thing. When I finally realized that the dark green shining mounds protruding from the body below the eye must be "nipples" I felt a sharp pain in my right breast and instinctively covered it with my hand but by then it was too late. My own nipple had split in two. I hurriedly pressed the two nipples back together and massaged them hard. As if that would have made the two one again. I actually must have created excessive pressure because the two nipples then split into four. The pain was intense. And I wanted to ignore it. With things like this on my mind I wouldn't be able to finish my work and in fact I hadn't even translated the first word yet. Coming to a faraway place apparently wasn't enough to break my habit of postponing work until the last possible moment. George once hinted in a round-about way that I always procrastinated not because I was lazy but because I was showing off insisting I absolutely

YOKO TAWADA

had to do things that I really didn't want to do in the first place. Deep down George never liked the idea of me translating anyway. He was always nagging me asking me why I didn't try something more physically active since I obviously wasn't cut out to be a translator. But I really couldn't understand why George loathed my translations and I was sure George didn't have the slightest idea why I hated him either.

. . . together, appear, those who kill, with the sacrifices, basically, always, only in a one-to-one ratio, never, come many, against one, to kill, for that, it continues, the appearance of, fair play . . .

"Thirteen more weeks and the dragon wind will be here. It pushes up from Africa and sometimes blows for days on end. You can't go outside. This is the best season," the woman in the shop said as she wrapped my goat's milk cheese and rye bread in wax paper. Her shelves were a jumble of laundry detergent and melons and weekly magazines in Spanish.

"Is it something like hot air? The dragon wind, I mean."

Realizing that I was ignorant of the dragon wind she explained angrily, "It's like an electric hair drier blowing on you all day. Just awful. Your hair starts to fall out and your face gets so dry the skin peels off in flakes. Nothing to do but cover your head with wet linen and crawl into a sleeping bag."

. . . nevertheless, brings, the killer, always, only, his own, self, with one, often, comes, he, high, on horseback, and, always, is he, safely, protected, covered, wearing armor, his attack power, is doubled, in a firm position, armed . . .

I tried to imagine the figure of a medieval knight mounted in armor but when the picture was finally complete in my mind the words I translated immediately destroyed the image. Better not to have a hero anyway I thought though I wasn't sure why I thought this.

"Oh, I see, it's the dragon-slayer legend. What made you choose that? Well, I guess it is universal in a way." When I talked to the editor on the phone I could tell from his voice that he wasn't very interested. "Saint George rides up, kills the dragon, rescues the princess—isn't that how it goes? There must be a contemporary twist, though, like the hero's really a coward or there's no dragon for him to slay. Or maybe it's the fair damsel who does the fighting. That seems more likely. Isn't this the age of feminism, whatever that means?" Feeling terribly insulted I retorted, "That's not it at all. Saint George really does fight the dragon. And the princess isn't a modern woman. I hate writers who change a few things around to get a simple solution. Why do you think I decided to translate the story instead of writing a new version of my own?" The editor naturally wasn't convinced and asked even more coolly, "Then what's so interesting about it?" I automatically answered, "Something *suddenly appears,*" but my enthusiasm was out of place and made it impossible for me to back down later.

. . . the sacrifices, on the other hand, appear, always, unprotected and bare, all alone, in battle, for defense, they, are wearing, their skin, will be carried, to market, desperately, frequently, on a tower, at the top, in a gable, on a column or landing, usually, half on the back, lying, brightly colored, vulnerable, belly, upturned, soft, in that place, the killer, stands, that is, still warm, animal-living, carpet, wearing riding boots, with spurs, comfortably, on the mat, in sinking . . .

Outside the window shadows were passing over the surface of the sea at an oddly leisurely pace. Looking up I saw the clouds rush by with surprising speed. I thought the banana grove had moved a little closer since this morning. I remember reading about a walking banana tree once. In the story the tree moved only at night. Not that the nearing banana grove really bothered me but merely for my own amusement I decided to count how many cacti I could see from the window. If I counted them now and remembered the number I could count them again later and then I'd be able to tell for sure whether the banana trees were really climbing up the slope little by little or if it only appeared that way. Plants don't interest me at all but if asked what kind was my favorite I think I would say cacti. I like them because they have no leaves and don't need water and besides they're not very useful. No matter how useless they may be though cacti stood between me and the banana grove and that seemed rather important to me just now.

I finally lost count. One of the toes on my right foot hurt so much I had to take off my slipper and take a look inside. Since arriving here pebbles kept getting in my shoes no matter how often I shook them out. It would be understandable if I was walking on gravel but right here in the house a sharp little stone crept into my slipper and tried to separate the flesh of my middle toe from the toenail. When I inspected my bare foot I discovered that the toenail was already purple from the bleeding underneath.

. . . wherever, people go, wherever, arrive, sacrifices, always, already, there, it is, so natural-seeming, there to be, like a monument, like a well, like a sidewalk or traffic light, therefore, in the same way, naturally, overlooked, passed over, much too, common motif, human, man, murderer, about to, one more, to another living thing, that concept, to show, about to strike a face, about to stab, about to poke a hole, about to smash, comes nearer, cuts off the head, that self, cannot protest . . .

Every time the sun peered through a break in the restlessly moving clouds the leaves of the palm trees by the house glittered like swords. There were moments when the tips fanned by the wind pointed straight at me. I wasn't particularly afraid of sharp objects unless my eyelids or the mucous membrane inside my mouth felt softer than usual. Then I'd become obsessed with the notion that other parts of my body were just as delicate and the sharp tips of even the most innocent leaves nearby looked disquieting.

. . . one victor, more, one sacrifice, more, one living thing, one animal, less . . .

"Do people ever come to the island on cargo boats?" I asked the woman in the shop.

"Recently, yes. Some men take them because they don't want to get their feet wet. The passenger boats are much safer than canoes and hardly ever leak. But they're no match for the trading vessels."

Saint George would definitely be afraid of getting his feet wet. Which was probably why he was always on horseback and those boots he wore must've sparkled from the massive amounts of oil he rubbed into them to keep water out.

"Are the trading boats so strong?"

"Of course they are. They use them for cargo, don't they?"

"What do you import in exchange for the bananas you export?"

"Mostly insecticides. For the banana grove."

Goat's milk cheese has the texture of soap and is nasty for the first bite but as the cheese sits in your mouth its peculiar flavor begins to permeate your tongue. Soon after coming to the island I forgot what cow's milk tasted like.

The same way cow's milk eliminates any trace of your mother's breast so it must be impossible to store lactic flavors in your memory bank. Goats are the only domesticated animal on this island.

"It's prohibited to import cows or birds or chickens, you know," said the woman gazing slyly at me from the corner of her eye. She talked as if she were certain I was in league with a gang of chicken smugglers and wanted to let me know she was on to me. I was annoyed and asked pointedly, "Is it also against the law to import eggs?"

"No, not as long as they're hard-boiled and the insides are thoroughly dead," she answered while taking a bottle of hard-boiled eggs out of the refrigerator to show me. The eggs were floating in the yellow liquid they'd been boiled in.

. . . the sacrifices, everywhere, since old times have been, their sin is what, serious, though, to them, congenital, error, undoubtedly, they, not human, are, they, different are, this alone, a misdemeanor, as the gravest offense, is regarded, and, ultimately, only, to be wiped out, particularly, if not to be turned into real coins, agreements for the protection of species, even, cannot lend a hand, supposing, at that time, already, such agreements, existed, because, they, to whatever species, do not belong, their own species, do not have . . .

I was walking in the dried-up riverbed with the author. If it weren't for the patterns the current and the aquatic plants had carved on both sides of the rocky banks and the stones under our feet worn smooth as *go* stones I could never have imagined that enough water to make a river once flowed here.

There was a man shiny with sweat gathering pebbles and putting them into a blue semitransparent vinyl bag as if he were collecting garbage. The bag was the same kind they used in the banana grove. We were about to pass him without so much as a greeting when he spoke: "In the rainy season the water comes back, you know." He looked straight at us waiting for a reply but I ignored him. "Come back after the dragon wind. There'll be water here, you'll see," he yelled after us refusing to give up. Here and there between the stones you could see damp earth. If you dug the earth with your fingers only a slight stink drifted up like a fart— no gushing streams. The deeper you went the wetter it became though there was no telling how far you'd have to go before you hit water. Since we hadn't brought a shovel or any other tools serious excavation was impossible. I had the feeling it would be utterly hopeless anyway.

"Let's go," the author said. We were walking on and on toward some indeterminate destination when I noticed a shadow neither wet nor dry constantly wavering back and forth across the stones. On closer examination I myself seemed to be casting the shadow as I walked though its shape was so distorted that it didn't look anything like me.

"If there was water here there would be no path," the author said. "Water would render it not a path but a river.

We wouldn't let that bother us, though. We'd simply have to walk somewhere else."

It suddenly occurred to me that she was terribly concerned about her age. So I needed to avoid saying anything like "But you don't look fifty" which implies there's something wrong with being that old. I didn't feel this way and in fact it no longer seemed possible that a woman under fifty could look beautiful. If I said nothing however the author would become more and more obsessed with her age. I tried to imagine what I'd say if she asked me why I had chosen to translate the work of such an old woman. Or if she told me she was too old to walk anymore. My fear was justified as the path narrowed and turned into a steep uphill grade. The author's breathing became labored and her every gasp sounded like the beginning of a question I'd have trouble answering and made my heart jump. Before long I too was panting and could only hear my own short breaths so I stopped thinking about age. I must have been thirsty. Otherwise I wouldn't have remembered the water bottle I had forgotten to bring.

The steep slope finally ended and the view in front of us opened up. We had apparently reached a grassy meadow halfway up a mountain. One peak loomed before us with another nearby. Unknowingly we seemed to have scaled quite a height for the flora had changed—the palms and cacti replaced with chestnut trees that covered the mountains. The sound of bells in the distance startled us. Far below we saw something black. Then brown and white patches appeared. Followed by pure white. Creatures of various sizes and colors were climbing up from the valley in a line. Goats. Each with a bell around its neck that rang in a different tone and engulfed the area in a strange amalgam of sounds. The tiny and terribly skinny black one at the front of the line made its way slowly up the path searching for footholds with thin gnarled legs.

"The weakest one always leads the pack," the author said. The line of goats continued without a break. One after another they trickled steadily out of the valley. Determined to see the goatherd and dog that would surely follow behind I trained my eyes on the procession without looking away for a moment. I felt like I wouldn't be able to relax until I had witnessed the "conclusion." Perhaps I was actually afraid of the goats. Or maybe I was jealous of their freedom to wander about the island without being bothered. If what people said about goats eating paper was really true I'd have to be careful not to let these itinerant beasts anywhere near my manuscript. I wondered if herding goats for a living made one jolly or gloomy. I was sure the author didn't have any desire whatsoever to see the goatherd. She would no doubt hate his dog even more. Nevertheless she kept her position beside me not moving from the spot.

Yet the last thing to appear was not the sort of "conclusion" I'd envisioned. At the end of the long line was a skinny little black goat just like the leader. With neither human nor canine companion the goats disappeared from sight with their bells still ringing.

"Wish I'd know from the start it would end like this," one of us said.

. . . they, do not belong, any species, to, a lineage, do not have, were, everywhere and nowhere, to be found, in water, on earth, or in, or under, in the air, they, always, solitary, from elsewhere, outsiders, ones like that, suspicion, excite, astonishing, so much, ill humor, arrogance, eccentricity, selfishness, his, unbridled, refusal to adapt, from a social standpoint, worthless, they, soon, begin to stink, in that way, they, the plague, bring, to everything, poisonous, odor, as in unofficial, records, in the Legenda Aurea, *literally, undecorated, is thus written, in addition, without salvation, that, outlandish, body, its existence, is shown, cannot be made, the idea, cannot be formed, the image, cannot be created, yet, painters, sculptors, poets, others, all, have tried, cannot be made . . .*

I thought I had seen a copy of the *Legenda Aurea* on the bookshelf the day I arrived so I went to look for it in the other room. The house contained only two rooms besides the kitchen. The one I used contained nothing but a desk and chair while the bookcase portable closet and bed were shoved into the other. The entrance to the bathroom was in the back of the house. My first day here I investigated the other room and had hardly entered it again since. A broken window frame rattled in there from time to time and I had the sense that someone was prowling around in the shadows behind me. The bed was soaked with the fragrance of cologne. I slept in my sleeping bag under the window beside the desk.

The bookcase was filled with a jumble of volumes left by previous guests. Of course there were the usual mysteries and pornography but I also found a scholarly study of the ecology of reptiles an introduction to Mesopotamian civilization a study of Kuwaiti women writers a computer catalogue and a book of traditional recipes from the Canary Islands. Reading the titles deepened my depression. Here was a pile of books I didn't want to read. I couldn't find the copy of the *Legenda Aurea*. Maybe I had confused it with Ovid's *Metamorphoses* which I did see on the shelves.

While I was looking at the bookcase I was overwhelmed by a strange desire to swim in the ocean. I imagined walking into the waves and squatting down to let the cold seawater rise up to my shoulders while only the soles of my feet planted firmly in the sand grew warm. I stretched my arms toward the ceiling took a deep breath and then wanted to jump into my bathing suit right away. But if I went down to the beach I would surely never finish the translation. I accepted the job because I wanted to so I better get busy and translate I repeated to myself. If it gets too frustrating I can easily quit but since I've never before had any trouble refusing work I found disagreeable and since I definitely didn't refuse this job I must not have had any objections for why else would I have agreed? I asked myself.

Sitting at the desk I started to wonder about this woman who thought she wanted to translate—who was she anyway? Last night I made the mistake of washing my hair with soap and the stiffened ends now pricked the back of my neck like twisted pieces of wire. I had forgotten to bring shampoo and the store didn't carry any. When I tried to use a rubber band to bind the hair in back the weight of the hair pulled at my skin causing my scalp to hurt every time I moved my head. I leaned forward and back searching for a position where my hair wouldn't jab the back of my neck without success.

Once again bothered by the gradually nearing banana grove I started to count the cacti. The rustling of the banana leaves seemed to be getting louder and though I thought the wind was picking up the palm leaves were still. Winds on this island seemed to blow down the hill in waves so it would often be quite breezy in front of the house and perfectly calm below. If someone else were here we might have talked about the cacti but I was sitting in the room by myself and not feeling the least bit lonely. If something happened to me one no one would be able to help anyway so I might as well be alone. Why did the doctor insist that I have a traveling companion? Both translation and thinking are things you must do on your own so I believe in the end I'm essentially always alone.

. . . shameless, shows, he, himself, his, equipment, than anyone's, better,

*united in one, all, every possible, accessory, specialized, or, unique, besides,
is thrifty, into only one, species, is divided into, a species of one, he, for
example, has, the claws of a wild cat, the fur of a bear, the skull of a
crocodile, the tongue of a snake, the skin of a lizard, the tail of an
American alligator, he, has, huge, bat wings, movable, armor of an
armadillo, and, sometimes, also, three eyelids, a nictitating membrane,
exactly, like a dog's, not at all, attempting to hide, his anus, above all, testicles, overripe, between his hind legs, sticking out, at the same time, pos-
sessing, on the same body, occasionally, in addition, breasts, or, several,
pointed, protruding, or, wantonly, hanging down, nipples, never before
heard of scandal, is, this leviathan . . .*

I thought I sensed something heave itself off the floor in
front of me. I stood up while taking a deep breath and was
about to speak but as I had nothing to say and no one to
say it to I sat back down again. Lots of little things to worried me. Moreover I remembered the internist warning me
not to see a doctor or drink tap water while I was on the
island.

I went through the manuscript blacking out all the masculine pronouns I had written. The creature had breasts. So
I couldn't use a word like "he" nor could I imagine what to
replace it with. Then again maybe the masculine pronoun
might really work. I vaguely remembered the Chinese character for "he" doesn't only refer to a man but can also mean
"the other side." The other side as a living thing called "he."
I went to the kitchen and split a tiger melon in half. I didn't

have anything else to eat. On the table I found a piece of hardened bread shaped like a canoe but I didn't want anything dry and I had already eaten the goat cheese. Though I could always walk down to the shop again I thought I'd better not leave yet. As I continued sitting alone in the kitchen the whole idea of translation became more and more incomprehensible.

"Unfortunately I can't say I'm proud of it," I answered when the man in the post office asked me what language I translated from. Knowing the islanders despised the language I really didn't want to tell him. Most of the tourists spoke it as their native tongue. "Then what language do you translate into?" was the next question and this time I openly replied, "My native tongue." The man must not have wanted to know what that was because he clammed up.

"The people here are all Spanish aren't they? There aren't any Africans or Arabs?" I asked in order to change the subject but this turned out to be another mistake.

"We are not Spanish. We are Canarians."

The two of us talked for a long time there at the only window in the only post office on the island. I felt something akin to nostalgia or the warmth of human contact for the first time since being here and then I had to blurt out something terribly practical.

"In three days I'll have to send my finished manuscript

by express mail so you'll be sure to open the post office at nine won't you?"

"Sending it express doesn't guarantee that it'll get there any faster you know," the man replied with a wink.

"That doesn't matter. Just so long as it leaves the island." The skin of a tiger melon like the fur of a tiger is yellow with black stripes. When you peel the skin off with your fingers plum-red flesh appears. The peel itself is so soft and tart and delicious there's really no need to remove it at all. But I was seized by an impulse to "rip it all off"—skin or anything else at hand. Maybe because of hunger. When I bit into the melon the juice dripped off my chin and dribbled between my breasts and beyond before collecting at the spot on my stomach that always breaks out when I catch a cold and that actually felt raw and itchy at the moment although I had no other visible symptoms. Reaching down to touch the spot would only make it worse. Meanwhile sitting here alone the itching became unbearable. Such distractions prevent me from progressing with my work. While finishing the translation might erase these little worries. Up to now I still hadn't ever finished translating a story. Some obstacle along the way always hindered me and I'd end up asking my friend Ei to translate the rest. I can't explain exactly what stopped me but for instance I'd catch a persistent cold and George would say things like, "That's why I keep telling you not to push yourself. You should turn down these silly translation jobs. You don't make any money from them anyway," and then I'd lose the will to continue. It was all George's fault. If it weren't for him I might be a stronger person.

Ei translates whatever I give her instantaneously and then tells me I should publish it under my name alone which makes me even more miserable. After becoming a successful novelist she didn't want to translate anymore and said she didn't want her name associated with my work. She seems to look down on translation. "Why don't you stop translating and write instead?" she says looking straight at me. "Translators don't count as artists you know." But I don't want to write novels. I translate because I want to not because I don't have the talent to be a novelist.

Which sounds very noble but with Ei always saving me these words don't mean much. For once I'd like to translate a story by myself though I fear the point of no return where I'll be forced into making unjust decisions as in the case of this story I'm certainly not Saint George and don't want to be though I feel in the end I'm the one who has to slay the dragon. "It's your own doing" someone might say and this beast *is* "my own doing" yet I'd also be the cause of the dragon's murder while I myself watched pale with horror like the princess in the story. Or I could be lying on the ground with my unsightly body stretched before the hero who ran me through with his sword. The mere thought of this makes me want to flee but there's no escape. No matter where I turned there would only be three roles to play: Saint George or the princess or the dragon. I could try to talk my way out. "I don't want to be any of them. I'm just the translator," I could say which might work for a bit until I was forced into another decision. Translation is a process of making choices. That's why I didn't want to complete this one. Nor did I want to give up in the middle   so I continued to slog on as usual.

Since mulling things over wasn't going to get me anywhere I thought a nice refreshing wash might perk me up and headed for the bathroom which wasn't so much a room as a space surrounded by four bare stone walls with one bucket and a length of thick rope inside. When you turned on the spigot in the corner the cloudy water that had collected in the tank during the rainy season trickled out. You collected the water in the tin bucket and washed yourself. I couldn't figure out what the rope was for. I poured the water in the bucket down my back cooling off my neck that stung from being jabbed by my own hair. Then I carefully washed my skin which the melon juice had turned red and raw. Like a sunbather my body looked the reddish-brown color of rust. My skin no longer seemed to be mine.

. . . product, from all, what crawls the earth, what flees, body, whatever precedent, or agreement, or classification, will not observe, body, outrageous, furthermore, division by sex, gender roles, ignores, that sort of, body, will perish, that alone, for a weapon, no wonder, people, he who is him-

self, wanting to get rid of, this body, in the end, forced to stop, shameless,
being this body, BE QUIET!, is told, sweating, STOP IT!, stinking,
STOP IT!, innocent lambs, maidens, eating, STOP IT!, not only that,
disappear, is told to, concerning that, opinions, are unanimous, he, already,
his own body, exploits, destroys, his rights, voluntarily, will not give up,
in that case, even if force is used . . .

"Ridiculous! Of course it isn't the banana grove that's dried out the island," the man at the fish market fumed. It was the same guy I had bought the tiger melon from. As there were no fruit stands here everyone bought their fruit at the fish market. Not that a truck the fishmonger drove around the island selling his wares whenever the fishing boat docked was a real market. "The dragon wind dries things up. In a few years, though, a bunch of engineers'll be coming from up north to build a huge seawall." Glowering at me he repeated, "That's nonsense blaming the banana grove." He made me want to complain some more about the banana grove but I bit my tongue then changed the subject to fish. Since he bought his catch from the fishing boat as soon as it docked and started on his rounds right away you'd think the fish would be very fresh but the boat traveled far into the open sea and returned with frozen salmon or halibut and sometimes even tuna already in cans.

"Fresh doesn't always mean the best taste you know. That's just a myth the tourists spread," he said.

"Can't you catch anything nearby?"

"You'll never eat a fish from the sea around here," he replied roaring with laughter. The darkness of his skin was different from that of the other islanders. At one time many laborers had emigrated from the Caribbean Islands and his father who was one of those laborers married a local widow and settled down here. When the man told me his parents had always wanted to get a divorce I didn't know what to say and instead bit my tongue again to restrain myself from asking if his father had worked in the banana grove.

. . . regrettable, for the leviathan, that, the leviathan's, actions, each one, unbearable to watch, absolutely, a chance, would have had, a little, kindness, if he had shown, soon, would have been made, a small protected area, according to the rules, gradually, where he can die, better yet, this, monster from, even, things to be harvested, must have been, for example, to shear, like sheep, to milk, colorful, feathers, one by one, to pluck out, a hide, to tear off, over the ears, in one piece, and then, eggs, to take, to fry, to boil, to freeze, to use, to make aphrodisiac . . .

Somehow I seemed to be losing speed. I was sure my pen was moving constantly and yet the amount I translated remained almost the same. Plus the more I worked the less I felt I knew what I was doing. How could this be a translation if the words didn't link up and even I couldn't understand what I was writing? Perhaps I should just forge ahead without rereading. Ei advised me to reread the whole manuscript several times from the reader's point of view but I can't put myself in another person's place step into their proverbial shoes. Of course this didn't mean I was locked inside myself unable to take anything in for I clearly sensed I was receiving something from the author. Nor was I not throwing back what I received either. What I was throwing and to whom was the mystery.

I kept throwing stones across the river. Though there was no water in the riverbed my feet were wet and cold. I saw a man on the opposite bank pick up the stones I had thrown and place them into a blue plastic bag. Every time my feet moved I could hear water splashing in my shoes which irritated me. I have nothing against water itself but the sound was excessively loud. I took off my shoes and shook them upside down. Dry pebbles tumbled out.

. . . the leviathan, only, slightly, just a little, given in, himself, under protection, of human beings, accepted, pretended to, swore his loyalty, only that, the leviathan, however, absolutely, would not do, the leviathan, stubborn, an enemy, continued to be, completely, no matter what, in principle, forever, and, in principle, forever, the leviathan, will not believe, in human beings, their words, himself, and them, will not get used to, pushes away, whatever approaches, without a syllable, but perhaps not, if there is one, only, a scream, a groan, a wail, wide enough to tear, opened, mouth, threatening, claws, and then, sometime, someone, thinks of, a pretext, just in time, when irritated, as always but, thinks of, a short procedure, to try out, thinks of an excuse, to the throat, with a spear, one thrust, to do, to

YOKO TAWADA

the face, one hit, with a lance, even then, yet, is not enough, on top of,
already, torn apart, with a sword, wildly, little by little, perishes, groans,
seep out, streams of blood . . .

The dogs on the island were as small as cats.

"We couldn't have dogs attacking the sheep, so the big ones and bad ones were put to sleep. And as the years went on . . . "

"So it must have been . . . "

"Natural selection!" The woman with frizzy hair stroking the ugly little dog in her lap exuded confidence. A woman with perfectly straight hair sat next to her with another little dog on her lap. They seemed to be close friends. In the evenings women like them lined chairs along the road to sit and talk while each held a little dog with its own kind of ugliness: bulging eyes or one ear that stuck straight up or enormous protruding testicles. During their puppyhood these dogs were free to roam the woods and often returned covered with burrs. A closer examination revealed that their back legs were firmly clamped between the women's thighs. The dogs wagged their tails but yelped occasionally perhaps in pain.

"Mine had a litter of brown puppies last week. Would you like one?" the woman with the frizzy hair asked me.

"No thanks. I only came here to translate."

"We have white ones too. And spotted ones."

"Any black ones?"

"No black ones."

There apparently wasn't a single black dog on the island. Because of the superstition that black dogs were the devil's messengers whenever a black puppy was born it was killed immediately.

"We get rid of those right away," the women said cheerfully.

. . . because, aggressors, Saint Michael, Saint George, for their occupation, angels, saints, they are, so, in other words, the Archangel, the Soldier of God, therefore, in attacking, they, perfect, backing, blessings, receive, succeed, always, new, order, create, this, disorderly, antisocial, inhuman, monster, this product, of godlessness, of chaos, that, far off, where it belongs, cast off, can never return, away, to hell, everlasting sin, to death, to the devil . . .

Of all the places I'd been on the island I liked the post office best. I did my relaxing there with the mail and not on the beach.

"Translation must be hard work," the postman said and I unintentionally ended up saying more than I wanted to.

"Yes it is. Because my skin's so tender. I have allergies."

"There's nothing unusual about that."

"That's what I always say."

"Are there any books that are never translated into another language?"

"Certainly. In fact most of the books in the world aren't."

"And are there some for which only the translations are left? Old books I mean."

"Sure. Sometimes the original disappears and only the translation is left."

"If there's only the translation then how can you tell it isn't the original?"

"Oh, you can tell right away. Because translation itself is something like a separate language. If the writing feels like pebbles falling down then you know it's a translation."

"You'd better not go down to the sea."

But the morning of the day he advised me not to go I had already gone. I sat on the sand between the seawall and the tourist hotels thinking about George. I don't know what started my ruminations which began before I realized it like a princess held captive on a deserted island waiting for a knight in shining armor to come to the rescue I reflected with a wry smile. One reason I wasn't the least bit like the princess in the story though was that I despised George so much I couldn't express it in words. Once I started to think about him an endless stream of thoughts would flow through my mind such as how great it would be if he didn't appear though there was nothing I could do to stop him now and if he did end up visiting how would I handle him when he got here?

Beyond the seawall was the port and from time to time a patch of industrial oil would float by shining on the water's surface like a rainbow. At nine o'clock a line of tourists trouped down to the beach. They all opened their bottles of suntan lotion at the same time and the whole place suddenly smelled like cologne. The odor reminded me of insecticide and made it hard to breathe so without thinking I stood up and ran toward the ocean. I splashed straight in with my clothes on. A piece of tissue floated in the water among clumps of reddish-brown seaweed. The seaweed wrapped itself around my legs. The moment I squatted down to pull the seaweed off I was caught by the force of the tide drawing back into the sea and fell over. The water I swallowed while I was lying there on my back wasn't salty but tasted like banana juice.

"Would you like one?"

The popsicle that the young ice cream vendor stuck under my nose was yellow and shaped like a banana.

"Is it organic?" I asked sharply. Whenever someone tries to sell me something I automatically turn nasty—a sort of self-preservation instinct.

"Naturally," he answered already giving up standing for-lornly in front of me. Two long slender deeply tanned legs poked out of his shorts. On his feet were women's beach sandals with colorful rubber poppies on them.

"Those are pretty sandals you've got on," I said without thinking. The ice cream vendor assumed an even gloomier look than when he'd heard the word "organic" but it was too late to take back my words. I felt awkward not being able to tell a pretty young man he looked pretty but I wasn't here to say touristy things and besides if I were selling ice cream and a tourist made that kind of remark to me I knew I'd be angry too.

By the time I said, "I'm sorry," he was walking away. It was a mistake to have come here in the first place. Sitting on a beach can make anyone look like a tourist sooner or later.

. . . again and again, countless, examples, can be given, for a cheap sideshow, a chance, as, are captured, are put on display, without shrinking in fear, without trying to hide, without being boiled in oil, without being killed, without being purified, bodies, are utterly useless, as a warning, in this place, the eternal, loser, unacceptable, bodies, ready-made, overcoats, cannot wear, bodies, every time, from the form, deviate, and, time and again, try twisting, try turning over, even then, unexpected, unnoticed, the compound eye, the facet of a gem, appears, sparkles, in any picture, captured, cannot be . . .

The slanting rays of the sun on the sand-colored slope transformed the cacti into guardsmen.

"Please don't let anyone in this house," I whispered to the cacti whom I trusted and respected more than people. Without any leaves to rustle no matter how hard the wind blew the cacti didn't make a sound. However a crowd seemed to have crept up behind them which could only be the banana trees jostling against one another. Assuming they were allowed out at night and had emerged from behind the fence they must be climbing the slope to see the sex show at the bar behind the planetarium. I had heard about the show from the doctor who said the audience would watch married couples indulge in long drawn-out sex on a tiny stage. Apparently there was nothing remarkable—no flashy displays of kinky technique. Of course the doctor hadn't visited himself though he seemed to enjoy recounting what his friend had witnessed.

I wondered if I should turn the light on. The thought of sitting at the desk translating while being a single bright spot on this dark island slope made me uneasy. Rather than being in the spotlight like a solo performer I preferred to hide behind the author where no one could see me and finish translating before anyone noticed.

"Seems someone's staying in that house."

"Seems she has allergies."

"Seems she's translating something."

"Seems she's cocky enough to eat tiger melons."

. . . all, is lost, but, powerful, shining iridescent, savagely, or, softly, with spines, with fangs, at the same time, light as a feather, blown away, in a tangle, interwoven, or, like a shadow, dark, bending down, or, with chest thrown out, it, is coming, before your eyes, into your heart, is coming, compared to it, heroically, with straightened back, is coming, the attacker,

YOKO TAWADA

eternally, will live, the attacker, how, commonplace, flavorless, is, only, he
himself, still, does not know, that, merely a plume, metallic, only the outer
covering, under that armor, just like type cases, drawers, many, are hid-
den, perhaps, and, the helmet, the cheek guard, behind, probably, a pale
weak face, is . . .

My fountain pen lightly touched the words of the original
text and smudged them with ink blots before wandering
through the air and landing on my manuscript to set down
in serpentine letters the words of my translation. My mind
was a blank so I simply let my hand move on its own. The
darkness obscured the letters forcing me to lean in closely.
Even with the window shut the rustling outside was incred-
ibly loud. Not wanting to turn on the light or speak and no
longer sure of what I was doing I continued to work. The
words transformed into holes. Not to say I was completely
numb or that I lost my will. I actually felt so full of curiosity that whenever I found a hole I stuck my hand straight
into it. I was walking with the author along the edge of a
volcanic crater after an eruption. The crater was a huge
bowl shaped like the traps antlions dig and was covered
with coarse black sand. The path we were walking on was
rimmed on both sides with boulders that looked like boil-
ing sewage. Holes in the boulders were the size of pine-
apples and my hand burned with pain each time I reached
into a hole causing me to scream. The author didn't seem to
hear me for she walked on without even bothering to turn

around. I deliberately slowed down to see if she would stop. Instead she walked even faster leaving me farther and farther behind.

"It's no use hurrying, because I can catch up with you whenever I want to. I may be a lousy swimmer, but running's my specialty," I said peevishly and watched the author climb into the crater. I saw her being drawn toward the center as her feet slipped deeper into the black sand. Letting the sand pull her down she talked to herself as she descended.

"The insurance salesman tells me it's time to give up and settle down. The eye doctor said the same thing when I asked him about bifocals. So did my old teacher when I happened to run into him at a funeral. I don't need advice like that. Yet my own mother gives it to me. While I took care of her when she said she was sick. With that smug director it was the same story. I don't need this shit. I really don't. I'm getting old, so everybody wants me to quit being a woman. Meaning to give up writing."

I considered following her into the crater but I was so scared of my feet sinking into the black sand that I couldn't move. Once I'm frightened of something my legs stiffen and I freeze. I have a cowardly streak and I fear both water and sand. I'm afraid of George and I'm afraid of work.

"Oh, I hate it, hate it, hate it," the author said as she sank. She definitely wasn't talking to me. She had forgotten I was there and was saying things I couldn't understand

Yoko Tawada

while she descended. The author obviously didn't need me. Whether the translator existed or not made no difference to her.

"Experience isn't something you build up—it's something you tear down."

"Please wait for me!"

"Don't give me that crap about my literary style. I write each page in a style I use only once so there's no such thing as 'my literary style.' I hate repetition. And I hate accumulation too." The author finally turned around and stared at me as though I were some passerby she'd never seen before and then without a sign of recognition she turned her back on me again. Being careful not to fall I scooped up a handful of gravel which I threw at her with all my might.

. . . and, the Princess, somewhere, safe, at a distance, the Soldier of God, in back of, the battle, shyly, with admiration, is watching, not qualified to speak, politely, with downcast eyes, only, can wait, and, to everything, devoutly, hoping, for her, the armor-clad man, on him, in attendance, for her, the savior, to her protector, to the master of her sex, does not forget her gratitude, so that, the monster, will go to hell, can only hope, that . . .

On several occasions I've wanted to say that I didn't find young women very pretty but as it always seemed I'd be misunderstood I held back. The author would probably suspect me of trying to make her feel better while really feeling superior about my younger age and my editor would definitely take it as sour grapes because I myself am getting older now and young women would think I was being rude. But I really do feel this way. Young women rarely look lively and most seem so stressed out you'd think they were "sacrifices." To compensate for their pale washed-out faces they hang slightly oversized ornaments on various parts of their bodies or suddenly appear one day wearing a little too much lipstick drawing malicious leers from others. Their skin looks cold and a hint of dark circles under their eyes suggests they've been crying through the night though you can see when they're making a ploy for sympathy by claiming to be utterly useless or trying to protect themselves by pretending to be terribly innocent. Far from evoking beauty these unconscious gestures are a malevolent social convention and whenever I see a woman in her prime I look forward to becoming like her as soon as possible.

. . . lipwork, the woman, is praying, is she not, not praying from the heart, because, the heart, the organ "heart," has gone somewhere, perhaps, has sunk, slipped down, to the bottom, beyond the hem of her slip, farther down than that, perhaps, tied up, and, like a sneak thief, is shivering, is quaking, the organ "heart," into the darkness, of the river of blood, is washed away, whirling round, of the deep green of fir trees, of purple, ankle-length, beautiful gown, below, and, furthermore, the organ "heart," of every, wrinkle, decoration, of seam, in back, over there also, if might be, of the dragon, of the apparition, of the monster, on the tongue, or, of

the throat, back, the murderer hero, time and again, time and again, takes aim, must pierce, of the throat, inside . . .

I cut through the fig grove to the street behind the house. This was a few days ago when I still didn't know where I could buy bread. For no particular reason I was convinced the shops were on higher ground so I trudged up the hill to look. The street if you could call it that wasn't paved but was flanked on both sides with stones and wide enough for vehicles to pass by though no matter how far I walked I saw neither cars nor people. Out of breath I stopped while a canary flew by and perched on a nearby shrub. The canary chattered away at a speed I couldn't hope to imitate. This was the first time I had seen a wild canary. I know almost nothing about birds and usually have no interest in them either. For some reason though I couldn't stop staring at this canary.

After a while I heard the sound of a car engine slowly drawing near. Without looking back I moved over to the left and kept walking leaving plenty of room for a car to pass. Perhaps the driver thought it was unnatural that I didn't turn around and react in some way because the hum of the engine grew louder and louder but the car itself didn't appear. I had heard that elderly people on the island thought it was rude to drive past a pedestrian. Most people didn't drive so fast anyway. Occasionally a young guy would rev up his motorcycle and end up plunging into the sea but besides this accidents were rare.

I felt weird looking back after so much time had passed so I continued to face forward. I could hear the sound of tires crunching on gravel and knew the car must be practically on top of me. Then I realized the road abruptly ended. Any direction that might have been called "forward" had completely disappeared into a steep slope above and below. The vehicle jerked to a halt. When I finally mustered the courage to turn around an angry-looking man with a towel wrapped around his head and something shiny in his hand stepped out. He was terribly tall and thin. He walked toward me without cracking a smile.

I almost screamed. Instead of attacking me he simply squatted at my feet. Keeping his eyes to the ground he took a broad plantain leaf in his hand and began cutting the leaf with his knife.

Relieved at first then feeling I had done something wrong I wanted to get out of his way and walk back but his truck blocked the path.

"I'll give you a ride when I'm done," the man said looking up. Sweat already dripped from his forehead. When he dropped the leaves one by one into a huge canvas bag the leaves seemed to disappear completely. He told me the leaves would be dried and fed to goats during the winter. The thought of standing there until the bag was full made me terribly anxious so I said, "I'm sorry but I can't wait that long."

In lieu of an answer he began telling me other things. He was studying physics at a university on the mainland and had returned to the island during break to help his parents. The fact that he was cutting plantain leaves certainly didn't mean he couldn't be a university student majoring in physics I told myself as I leaned against the truck watching him work. I didn't want to help him as I don't like touching plants with my bare hands nor did I want to squat next to him.

"Here for travel? Or whoring?" I couldn't believe my ears but that was definitely what he said.

"Neither."

"Oh? But you sure look like her," the man said looking straight at me. I didn't want to ask him who and then have to talk about her.

"I've come to translate," I said trying to steer the conversation away from troublesome topics.

The man looked bored as he turned away and said, "You have an easy life." Mere coincidence no doubt but George always said this to me too. And whenever he did it robbed me of my courage and sapped my strength leaving me upset but too weak-kneed to really get mad. Perhaps finding my long silence strange the man looked up. A glimmer of piercing curiosity crossed his face. Pretending not to notice

I climbed over the dusty hood of the truck and without saying good-bye walked back along the road.

. . . the organ "heart," no more, must not, beat, pump blood, pulsate, must not, the heart's pain, all ceased, must be, at least, under the bridal veil, of desire, swamp, all dried up, just like George, from the start, parched, of the flesh, desire, from him, far away, has stayed, as is, in the official report, written, water, and, tears, dried . . .

By the windowsill a lizard the color of rusty scissors scurried away. Outside it was pitch black so I couldn't see cacti or palm trees or even a single banana tree. I did hear the banana leaves rub against each other now and then like people whispering which was disturbing to listen to in the dark for it seemed like I wasn't alone in the room. When I turned on the light the hissing voices faded for a while only to gradually return. I must have been in full view from the outside.

"I just have a little more to do so please be quiet."

The undertone intensified into a cacophony. I went into the kitchen and cooled my forehead with water from the sink. And as I didn't have anything else to drink I took a little sip of the water though I knew I shouldn't have. I became very sleepy.

"Don't sleep."

"If you do you won't be able to tell what sort of face it is anymore."

"Even if you do you might make it in time."

Was the wind planning to blow all night? Or perhaps it wasn't blowing at all. As I began to hear the strange voices more clearly the letters before my eyes blurred becoming less and less readable.

. . . inside, shut away, Virginal, princess, of life, from one stage, another, stage to, shrinks, but, almost, hidden, and, in a trance, seemingly, at all costs, she, to something, fast, wants to hold on, seems to, and, to the dragon, namely, is holding, little by little, to its own death, advances, the dragon, groaning, stocking, or, belt, is, of that cord, one end, of the dragon, neck, is wrapped around, the other, end, is holding, she, with both hands, both hands, to the same cord, are holding on, by that cord, she, the dragon, or, the dragon, her, to the city, will take, will be taken, in the city, with one stroke, will lose its head, and, she, will be baptized . . .

My face was an indistinguishable blob reflected in the glass. In the center of the blob a light flashed.

"Please don't look in."

My thirst was making me irritable. As the window rattled I heard what sounded like a crowd of people whistling.

"If you're the wind come back when you sound like it."

A burst of laughter. At me no doubt. I scratched furiously at my right elbow. The skin broke and my fingertips turned red with blood. I picked up the dirty towel that had fallen to the floor and rubbed my fingers and elbow hard as if I were grating Parmesan cheese.

"Filthy."

"She doesn't seem to mind."

"Seems to be doing it on purpose."

Clinging to the desk I translated the final words.

. . . in oil paintings, or, as statues, lifted up, the dragon, already, terribly, beaten, head, looks back, as if, still, a chance, to say, toward the murderer, a wide open mouth, a mouth filled with blood, just like a wound split open, with that mouth, will never be healed, will never be closed, that mouth, roars, that cry, and, bellowing, groaning, words of the body, words of the heart, in the painting, ancestral, made dumb.

I ran into the kitchen and drank glass after glass of tap water. Then I laid my head on the kitchen table planning to rest for thirty seconds. On the count of thirty I would fold up the two pages put them in an envelope and write the address.

But when I counted to thirty and stood up dawn was breaking. Shocked I returned to the desk to find the pages as I had left them. I looked out the window and saw that the banana grove had receded to the horizon. The crimson cloud floating in the eastern sky looked like a scab—a hard ripe one ready to be torn off. I quickly folded the manuscript and put it in an envelope. Then suddenly wondering why I had folded the pages into a triangle I opened the envelope again and discovered I had folded them into a square after all but the title was missing. You might say this was perfectly natural since translating the title had completely slipped my mind.

"Will phone in the title tomorrow." As I scrawled this in a corner with my fountain pen a troubling thought occurred to me. "You mustn't under any circumstances use a refillable ink pen," the editor had said over the phone. "Why not? I'll send the manuscript airmail you know so it won't fall in the water," I answered. Ei later told me he thought I was being sarcastic. When he saw the manuscript he would no doubt think I used this kind of ink on purpose just to irritate him. And there was no way I could copy the whole thing over again. The man at the post office would surely be waiting for me with the window open at nine and I'd feel terrible if I let him down. He was the only person on the island I thought might understand my work and I couldn't betray him for a little thing like the wrong kind of ink. What was wrong with fountain pens anyway? I thought ready to fight. My ink was fine. If it was going to smear let it smear. If it disappeared altogether that would be fine too. Besides I had more important things to worry about than ink. I kicked off my bedroom slippers only to find my shoes weren't outside the door. Perhaps the neighborhood children had stolen them. I tried to recall why I had left them out there yesterday of all days but even if I remembered I knew it wouldn't do me any good and then it came to me. I had gotten water in them. My shoes were soaking wet so I had left them outside to dry. But how had I gotten my feet wet? I didn't have any memory of a river that wasn't dried up. On this island I haven't even seen a riverbed with water in it. No use thinking about that either. The water shortage was tied up with the whole issue of trade and there was nothing I could do about it. If they wanted to save water they would have to stop exporting bananas which in turn would stop foreign currency from pouring in thus bringing an end to the import trade.

I dashed through the house opening all the cupboards. On the bottom shelf of the dish cupboard I found an iron pot big enough to boil a baby goat with a pair of red felt shoes a copy of the *Legenda Aurea* and the key to the cellar hidden inside. There's no escaping the eyes of someone who knows to look in unexpected places I thought feeling pleased with myself. The red felt shoes looked familiar. I had seen shoes like that on the feet of a princess in a Paolo Uccello painting in the London National Gallery. Saint Michael also wears a pair as he stamps on a snake. In that painting by Piero della Francesca the look in Saint Michael's eyes made me shudder. Crushing a snake . . . The shoes stomping the poor creature to death . . . I couldn't bear to put them on. I was horrified that the cruel dissipated dissatisfied look in Saint Michael's eyes would eclipse my gaze. Being infected with the expression on the princess's face would be even more horrifying. Even without her corrupting influence I was sure I had once looked like her at one time or another. I probably wasn't aware of it either. Which made it more revolting.

I had no choice but to put on the red felt shoes. Then I picked up the envelope and was about to leave when I realized I didn't have the house key. When the cellar key had come out of hiding the house key must have disappeared in its place. This is the way things work with natural selection and trade balance or trade selection and natural balance. They let you rejoice at having found one thing when actually they're hiding the fact that something else has disappeared. There was no time to look for the door key. George might have been on the first trading vessel that arrived this morning. Or perhaps he would be on the first plane. Before that happened I simply had to get this translation to the post office.

BACK IN FIVE MINUTES. I scribbled these words on a piece of paper and stuck it on the door. Telling myself that this note would let thieves know how soon they could expect me back so they wouldn't be able steal anything I started down the slope. Then another worrying thought occurred to me. Now anyone could know I wasn't home. People who weren't aware of my presence before would know that I'd stepped out for a moment. Of course there was no time to climb back up the slope to remove the note. The man at the post office might get mad at me for not showing up and close the window. Maybe he would decide that translators couldn't be trusted after all. I noticed a woman with frizzy hair sitting by the side of the road holding a little dog. I had spoken with her once before so I felt like I knew her.

"Won't you take a brown puppy off my hands?" she asked without a word of greeting.

"I hate to ask you this but there's a piece of paper on the door of the house by the palm tree. Would you mind getting rid of it? If it's not taken down I'm afraid something terrible will happen. I'd do it myself except I'm in a huge rush." I knew I was being presumptuous but there was no else to ask.

"How nasty of you!" the woman laughed slapping her knees once with both hands. She had every right to react this way. I had only my own carelessness to blame. If a thief broke in and took the iron or the electric carving knife I would have to pay for it. The worst thing is I'd have to tell the police who I heard always spent several painstaking days investigating a case. So little happened on the island that they wanted to leave the most thorough record possible of every incident no matter how minor. And I can't stand being interrogated about my private life. They'd probably start out by asking why I hadn't brought my husband along and when they found out I didn't have one they'd want to know why and what sort of relationship I had with the single doctor who owned the house. If he wasn't my lover then why was he letting me use the house? What would I do to repay him? If I was here to translate then how much of a royalty was I receiving? If there was no royalty then how would the editor compensate me for my work? Perhaps *he* was my lover? Or a former lover? And if not then which flight would my real lover arrive on? And if not my lover then who exactly was this George I was expecting by boat? How many times had I slept with him? If our relationship wasn't physical then how deep was it? And if there was no relationship then why not? What had kept us from developing one? These matters were clearly under police jurisdiction. If a man showed up to ask such questions I'd immediately know he was a cop even if he wasn't in uniform. That's how sensitive I'd become to the way the police worked and the kinds of questions they asked. Once they had me where they wanted me not only would I not be able to translate literature anymore I'd be sure to lose every refuge that existed in my daily life. With no time to explain everything to the woman holding the little dog and not knowing how to anyway I sprinted down the slope without saying anything.

"Hey, you there! Stop! Wait a minute!" the owner of the general store yelled as I passed by. I didn't have time to chat but the smell of goat's milk wafting from the shop made me so hungry I was sure I'd never make it to the post office if I didn't eat something so I relented and walked inside and immediately grabbed a piece of goat cheese and shoved it into my mouth. Then I realized my wallet was back at the house. I wanted to cry. Without my wallet I wouldn't be able to buy stamps at the post office. And if I went back to get it the post office would close. I really did burst into tears. When I finally looked up the woman was watching me with great interest. As she was trapped in the shop every day of the year incidents like this must be her only source of amusement. Plus there's something undeniably fascinating about watching someone cry so it's nothing to get upset about I thought as I stood there teary-eyed until I eventually realized that although I was crying I didn't feel the least bit sad. I proceeded to explain everything to the woman from beginning to end and when I finished she went to the back of the shop fetched an imported tea can and placed a handful of bills from the can into my hand.

"Here. I'll lend you this." The bills were disconcertingly slick and so light that I thought I was holding children's play money. But it was better than nothing. And she was definitely trying to help. It didn't matter why. Perhaps she didn't have a reason. Maybe she was bored. Clutching the bills and wondering why I felt absolutely no sense of gratitude I left the shop.

As I ran along the road by the banana grove I remembered the man in the straw hat leaning against the wall who had asked me in a sarcastic tone, "Think you'll make it in time?" He obviously couldn't have understood what he was saying despite having a knack for perceiving the crux of the matter. Yet now if I could only keep this pace up without falling I was sure to make it in time. I ran. On the way I passed the deserted beach. I was astonished to see a boy of about seven using an evil-looking metal toy sword to hit what looked like a stone beside the changing stalls. Holding the envelope tightly to my chest I walked over to him. I simply couldn't let him continue. For as I walked closer I saw that as I had suspected he was striking not a stone but a living thing—a turtle with its head and legs drawn in. I took hold of the boy's hand from behind and gently squeezed. I wanted to speak to him but didn't know what to say. His hand was hot and sticky. He looked up at me and pinched my cheek wrenching the flesh upward.

"OUCH!" I screamed without thinking. He actually didn't mean to hurt me. I didn't know this at the time but harming me was the farthest thing from his mind.

"Your cheek had some dirty skin on it," he said in perfect innocence. He was only trying to clean me up. He had seen a smudge on my cheek and wanted to rip it off. Not comprehending that skin doesn't come off so easily he was only acting out of kindness. He then turned his attention to the envelope I was holding to my chest and stared at it as if he were appraising its value. Sensing danger I intentionally lowered my voice and said, "Let's go peek in the stalls. There's bound to be lots of pretty ladies changing inside." It was a foolish thing to say and I felt utterly disgusted with myself. Showing absolutely zero interest the boy continued to eye my envelope. I gave his back a shove and pushed him over to one of the stall doors.

"Come on. Let's look inside. It'll be fun. You can see everything, you know." I pushed him so hard into the empty stall that he fell face down on the floor and after slamming the door shut behind him I piled some heavy stones against it. I was positive he couldn't escape. Small as he was he already had the air of Saint George about him. Which was why he wanted to steal my envelope. He could bang on the door as much as he liked but he was in there for good. Maybe his nose was bleeding. Now I can go to the post office I thought with a sigh of relief.

As I cut across the beach I saw the ice cream vendor coming toward me in the distance. By the time I wondered why he was selling ice cream this early in the morning it was already too late. He was in front of me and with a confident smile lifted a bronze sword from the ice cream cart. He looked so much like the little boy I asked myself how the boy could have grown so fast. I couldn't physically overpower him this time. My first instinct was to look down demurely. The young man placed his left hand on my shoulder. His right hand still held the sword.

"I don't see how I can do it alone," I said praying he wouldn't notice the envelope I was holding behind my back.

"Sure you can," he replied while clumsily but tenderly stroking my hair. I could tell it wasn't my hair but my skin he wanted to touch. One of his fingers tried to slide into my ear but it was too fat and slipped along my shoulder onto my bare upper arm down to my elbow. "Your skin's gotten so rusty," he said looking quite happy. I wasn't sure what he was trying to imply though it couldn't have been anything good.

"Because I'm getting old. You're lucky you're still young," I answered carefully. If he read my mind everything would end I thought not knowing what I meant by this.

"Oh, I wouldn't say that. You've matured, that's all. Your skin might start peeling off, you know," he said lightly touching my arm with the blade of his sword. Though I can't say I felt any pain a narrow strip of skin peeled off and hung from the tip of the blade. Red spots appeared on my naked flesh where blood welled to the surface. I felt ashamed of the spots.

"I really admire you. You have what it takes to get things done on time. I don't even start until the last possible moment. But once you start you always stay focused, don't you? I can't. My mind wanders, so . . ." Doubts lurked in the back of my mind as to why I had suddenly launched into this self-accusing monologue. Perhaps it was a defense mechanism.

"I have so little ambition that no matter how hard I work I end up going around in circles. You stand out in a crowd so nobody has any trouble remembering your name. People forget mine as soon as they hear it. The work I do really isn't difficult for anyone with decent language skills but the talented ones don't want to waste their time with dumb jobs like mine. I envy you. I bet you decided what you wanted to be when you were still a kid. And once you made up your mind, you never wavered."

"Forget it. It's too late for flattery," the youth said unswayed. Every time he touched me with the blade my reddish-brown skin turned purple. He seemed determined to flay my whole body that it was something he felt he absolutely had to do for my sake.

"There's nothing to worry about anymore," he whispered twice. Though he did look a little embarrassed he was obviously proud of his handiwork. I couldn't move and my mind became completely empty. This was only natural as I was trapped in the embrace of the Saint George I hated so much. I was suffocating and I knew I had to run away quick with my envelope.

"You're going to be all right," said the youth gently.

When I replied with the first thing I could think of he gasped and pushed me away. "What about your horse? Look! Over there! It's getting away. You must've forgotten to tie it up." I saw the shadow of a horse galloping along the sea wall. The young man swung around and raced off in that direction. He was so spry and quick he could only have been Saint George even if he had lost his horse. I ran up the hill toward the post office.

I was almost there when I saw another Saint George blocking my way. He was smiling with his arms stretched out across the entire width of the road. Unlike the youth he was a little pudgy.

"Give me the envelope now. I know you have it." I sank down into the street. My knees felt so weak I couldn't muster the strength to stand up again. The man rolled his eyes and said, "Aw, come on. I didn't mean it that way. I was only joking. You shouldn't take everything I say so seriously. I was just a little upset with you. You did lie to me about your travel plans, didn't you? That made me mad. But it's nothing to worry about. Everything's going to be fine."

What he said was true. I had lied to everyone about my schedule even saying that I would be flying to a completely different island. I knew I was in trouble when I bumped into George's best friend at the airport.

"Get up now. It's okay. Let's be friends and go have a cup of espresso together."

Taking my arm the man pulled me up into his fleshy chest and we started to walk. Suddenly enveloped by the fragrance of eucalyptus I looked up and was startled to see a single tree standing by the side of the road looking down on us. Perhaps everything *was* fine. I began to feel it might be. I could forget about my envelope and let nature take its course.

We went into the café behind the post office. The moment we opened the door the men sitting at the bar turned around to look at us. The scent of papaya liqueur floated in the air.

"Must've been so hard for you," said the man as he put a hand on my shoulder and began sucking on my earlobe. The men at the bar turned away.

"Oh, I don't know about *so* hard . . ."

"But you must have been lonely."

"I had the islanders to talk to. And besides I had my work."

"You have an easy life."

"Work is work."

"You don't need to worry anymore."

"I wanted to translate something to the very end."

"You have an easy life."

"What did you say?"

"You'll never do it. But why don't you forget all about it now?"

"My shoulders got stiff."

"People whose shoulders aren't stiff are nicer."

"Because I didn't have enough time."

"But it's over now so there's nothing else you can do."

"This morning I was so busy I didn't even have time to go to the bathroom. I really don't have time."

"Isn't our espresso ready yet?"

"Excuse me." A strange passion gripped me in the chest and I stood up. I had to act now. Perhaps there was still time. But if I let this chance slip by there would never be another.

The bathroom was behind the counter. As soon as I entered the flies flocked to the moisture on the back of my neck. They greedily sucked up my sweat and every time I shooed them away they would rise into an arc and fly right back again. As I expected there was a window with frosted glass at the back. I pushed the window open and climbed out falling headfirst to the other side. I landed in a sort of garbage dump where the chill of rotten fruit peelings clinging to my neck drove the flies away at once. In a panic I struggled to get up but moved too quickly so that I tipped sideways causing my head to squish into something soft like tar—a black and sticky substance impossible to get out of my hair or off my fingers no matter how much I pulled. As I couldn't find a firm foothold whenever I tried to stand I sank into a swamp-like morass. Among soggy pieces of cardboard at the cusp of complete disintegration rolls of brown wrapping paper were still dry and crisp enough to crackle furiously. Finally I steadied myself on a wooden crate and was able to stand up.

The garbage dump led into the post office's back garden which I crossed to find a bicycle rack with a single bike beneath a lone palm tree and a door almost hidden by the tree. The door wasn't locked.

The floor of the post office was soaked. Dirty scraps of paper floated in the scattered puddles of muddy water. Near the front entrance was another Saint George in tall rubber boots stabbing something over and over again with what looked like a fencing rapier. The "something" was reddish-brown as small as a cat and as amorphous as a piece of doormat. Brown water splashed around as it either resisted or tried to escape or perhaps wasn't alive after all. Saint George seemed almost bored the way he half-heartedly sawed back and forth with his sword but then he would suddenly bare his teeth and thrust with a vengeance. Whenever he let out an occasional groan or cheer the "something" was silent. Nothing happened. And it looked like nothing ever would. Nevertheless Saint George diligently continued to move his sword back and forth.

"Where's the man who works here?" I asked. Without stopping to look at me Saint George answered politely, "He's gone home." I reached behind the counter and opened a box full of official airmail and express mail seals which I rummaged through for a while before remembering I was actually looking for stamps. I couldn't find any in the box. I had to send this envelope immediately and there were no stamps! I looked more closely at the "something" that was thrashing around in the dirty water.

"That is not my skin is it?" I asked.

"Of course not," answered Saint George elegantly with a merry laugh.

Then I realized something truly horrifying. The envelope was gone. What I was holding in my hand was not the envelope but a piece of wet carpet. I must have dropped the envelope in the trash heap and picked up this useless rag instead. Throwing the soggy carpet to the floor I rushed into the garden. As I ran for the dump I saw someone standing ahead of me blocking my line of vision. It was the previous Saint George with a demitasse of espresso in each hand. Steam rose from the cups.

"Where were you?" The gentle voice from before was replaced with a frightening growl deep within his throat. "Why did you climb out the window?" I whipped around in the direction of the post office. This was no situation I could bluff my way out of. I was off on a good running start when my ankle cracked and I nearly collapsed.

"Fall!" commanded a deep voice from behind. But I didn't fall. I ran into the post office. The Saint George of a moment before was gone. In his place was a puddle of deep red water. Splashing through the puddle to the front door I burst into the street. My shoes were wet and about to fall off as the laces were loose but I couldn't stop. As I ran toward the beach my shoelaces trailed behind me.

I chose that direction because it was a downward slope. I didn't have the energy to climb up so I ran down letting my legs move mechanically right foot forward first then the left foot. In time I would reach an expanse of sand. If I didn't stop I'd reach the sea which would be another dead end. Hemmed in on each side by seawall and lodging houses I'd be unable to flee in any direction except forward straight into the sea. I probably wouldn't choose this though seeing how I could only swim a distance of twenty-five meters. If not into the water then where else could I escape? I wouldn't know until the ocean loomed before my eyes. How much further was it? Far away or really quite near? With these and many other questions on my mind I ran on down the slope.

Translator's Afterword

Facing the Bridge is Yoko Tawada's third collection of stories published in the United States. Tawada, who writes in both German and Japanese, is not nearly as interested in crossing borders as she is in the borders themselves—the spaces in between that are hidden by conventional bridges, including official channels of communication (she has a profound mistrust of words like "information" and "communication"). So in the title of this volume she chooses to face the bridge, to stare it down, perhaps, refusing to cross. Through her writing she seeks to create a new kind of bridge—not as a structure built of stone or concrete, but as a physical process, a continuing dance.

In Tawada's play *Till*, a group of Japanese tourists on a guided tour through the Niedersaxon region of Germany encounter the medieval trickster Till Eulenspiegel. The play was performed in Germany and Japan (I saw it in Tokyo), with the actors speaking either German or Japanese according to their roles, which meant that the majority of the audience in each country could understand only half the dialogue. The Japanese guide—the only character proficient in both languages—initially acts as her tour group's "bridge" to the foreign culture, dispensing information about wine, hotels, and German society in general. Until Till appears, that is, bringing in his wake a number of stock characters from medieval Germany—a blacksmith, a butcher, and a landowner—plus an assortment of more bizarre types, including a woman with a third eye in her forehead, a motley group with mushrooms growing out of their heads, and mysterious dog-headed figures. The guide continues to expound on the position of the craftsman in medieval society, but as her information is now useless (who needs a lecture when there's a medieval blacksmith standing in front of you?) she is duly ignored. As the guided tour disintegrates, the actors run, leap, and glide across the stage until it seems they are indeed dancing their way to a new sort of bridge.

Travel as a state of being in between places is a major motif in Tawada's work; like the tour group in *Till*, the characters in the three stories collected here are all travelers. The stories were originally published in three different books, but I thought it would be interesting to place the narrator of "Saint George and the Translator," who rejects the idea of tourism altogether ("I only came here to translate!" she says) side by side with Kazuko of "In Front of Trang Tien Bridge," who is so dedicated to tourism that she identifies herself as "a member of the tourist race." The question of race, in its more conventional sense, figures most prominently in the first story, "The Shadow Man."

Both Amo and Tamao of "The Shadow Man" are reluctant travelers. As is well known in Germany but perhaps less so in the United States, Amo was a real person, known as Anton Wilhelm Amo, or simply Amo of Ghana. Brought to Europe by Dutch slave traders early in the eighteenth century, he spent much of his childhood in the palace of Anton Ulrich, the Duke of Braunschweig-Wolfenbüttel, to whom he was given as a present. The Duke and his son Wilhelm sponsored Amo's studies first at the University of Halle and later at the University of Wittenburg, where he was awarded a doctorate in philosophy for a dissertation entitled *On the Absence of Sensation in the Human Mind and its Presence in our Organic and Living Body.* He taught philosophy both at Halle and Jena, but after the deaths of his patrons he became increasingly vulnerable to vicious racist attacks and eventually returned to his homeland, where he is thought to have died in a Dutch fort—imprisoned, some say, to prevent him from inciting protest among his people—sometime around 1759.

Amo's writings, especially *On the Rights of the Moors in Europe*, are thought to have influenced Gotthold Ephraim Lessing, the poet and philosopher of the German Enlightenment who moved to Wolfenbüttel in 1770 to work as a librarian. This seems ironic in light of the fact that, like all Europeans, Lessing is a descendent of the "Bad Spirits" that surround Amo during his life in Europe. However, in "The Shadow Man," European humanism means no more to Amo than it does to Tamao, who takes nationalistic pride in the cherry tree in front of Lessing's house, blissfully unaware that most Germans certainly do not see it as a symbol of Japan. Whereas Amo finally finds a sense of identity through the painful discovery that he was brought to Europe on a slave ship, Tamao dreads being identified with other Asians, and even more so with Amo, despite his admiration for Michael Jackson: "When he watched Michael Jackson's videos, every cell in Tamao's body started to seethe: he even felt his appearance begin to change." In this desire to dissociate himself from his own identity, Tamao has much in common with the Japanese of his generation, for whom "Asia" is a common tourist destination, and who are often shocked to find that many Americans still see Japan as the *Oriento* ("Orient" in

Japanese), an "exotic Asia" that has never existed.

When I read "The Shadow Man" with my students at a women's university in Tokyo, many said they knew someone like Tamao—a budding scholar who aspires to academic success by following in his professor's footsteps, who masks his insecurity with what he thinks are clever wisecracks, and to whom the idea of a female rival is particularly unbearable. Burdened with useless information provided by an older friend (*sempai*) who has advised him against studying abroad in the first place, Tamao is no more comfortable in Europe than Amo was nearly two centuries earlier. The enigmatic Manfred reminds him of this fact, irritating him all the more. Ironically, Manfred's disappearance brings Tamao and Nana together. Through the physical act of running while in pursuit of Manfred, a new bond forms between them, much as Amo's only connection with a European woman—his housekeeper's daughter, Marguerite—was made through the dance they shared while putting on his coat. Yet whether or not Tamao and Nana's truce will prove any more permanent than the tenuous "bridge" between Amo and Marguerite remains an open question.

We can assume that Kazuko of "In Front of Trang Tien Bridge" attended university during the late '60s or early '70s, when protests against the Vietnam War were at their height. Resentment at Japan's involvement in the war through the U.S.-Japan Security Treaty and the presence of American military bases on Japanese soil fueled anti-American sentiment during this period. Antiwar slogans in a distinctive, angular style of calligraphy appeared on homemade signs and billboards on campuses across Japan, with students in jeans and helmets standing in front of the signs screaming through megaphones in voices so over-amplified they were often unintelligible.

Perhaps to capture the cacophony of the student movement, Tawada has an androgynous figure shout a series of phonetic syllables at Kazuko that look as though they should mean something but are actually nonsensical. Rather than assigning them an arbitrary meaning in the translation, I have transcribed them, preserving the grammatical structure of the Japanese text.

The photograph Kazuko observes in the War Remnants Museum (until recently called the Museum of American War Crimes) was taken by the Okinawan-born photographer Ishikawa Bunyo. It is one of the images in Harrell Fletcher's exhibition The American War (the Vietnamese name for what Americans call "The Vietnam War"), which toured the United States during 2006, and can now be viewed on Fletcher's website (www.harrellfletcher.com/theamericanwar/). Ishikawa says in his caption to the photo that the American GI "laughed satisfactorily while carrying a part of the body of a liberation soldier. . . ." I would like to believe Michael Kimmelmann when he suggests in his review of Fletcher's exhibition that the soldier does not immediately appear to be laughing ("'The American War': Harrell Fletcher's Vietnam Photographs at the White Columns," in *The New York Times*, June 5, 2006), but this may be due to a last-ditch effort to convince myself that although Americans may be capable of such atrocities they would not laugh while committing them—a negative form, perhaps, of Kazuko's "twisted pride" when she wants everyone in the museum to notice the photograph was taken by someone Japanese.

Faced with the aftermath of the Vietnam (or American) War, Kazuko is suddenly aware of herself as a Japanese. Although she has been mistaken for a Vietnamese in both Berlin and Ho Chi Minh City, when she sees a lean, sinewy soldier emerge from a hole in the ground outside the Cu Chi Tunnels, she realizes that even though she is Asian her body doesn't look Vietnamese after all. The weight of history intensifies her feeling of difference as the pride the Vietnamese obviously take in their victory leads her to reflect on the war that Japan lost to America. During the final months of that war, Japanese civilians were required to practice using bamboo spears in preparation for an anticipated American invasion, to be met with the "shattering of the jewel" (fight to the death) of the "million hearts that beat as one." (This aspect of wartime experience is conspicuously absent from the National Showa Memorial Museum, the purpose of which is, according to the museum's English pamphlet, to "convey the life of Japanese during and after the World War II." Nor do any of the museum's many exhibits mention the fact that for Japan, WWII began as a war of aggression in Asia.)

Once inside the Cu Chi Tunnels, Kazuko is gripped with a terror so intense that she feels alienated from herself; with her sense of self about to disintegrate, the concept of national identity—Japanese or Vietnamese—becomes irrelevant. What saves her from total annihilation is the appearance out of nowhere of the words "all right," which effectively dissolve the net of fear that has enveloped her. In Tawada's writing, words broken down into their basic elements often have an almost mystical, spell-breaking power (the word *daijobu*, which I have translated as "all right" is written phonetically in the angular *katakana* script that is normally used to write foreign words and, often, onomatopoeia in manga). I am reminded here of a similar scene in the story "The Gotthard Railway" (published in *The Bridegroom Was a Dog*) in which the narrator feels that she has "gone blank" in the sheer whiteness of a snowy field, and is unable to move. Only by chanting "Göschenen," the name of "the ugliest town in Switzerland," which the narrator describes as "a word made of stone," does she recover her lost self and begin to walk again.

The final scene of "In Front of Trang Tien Bridge" reminds me of a haiku by the poet Nagata Koi: "Split into several selves I go my separate ways." People often speak of traveling in order to find themselves, and in a sense, Kazuko has done just that as everyone on the tour bus is her. Throughout the story, it has been difficult to tell who is who. In Berlin, where many think "Asia is all in one place," the Japanese use signs of conspicuous consumption, such as jewelry and brand-name handbags, to distinguish themselves from the Vietnamese. In Ho Chi Minh City, on the other hand, Kazuko discovers that though she looks Vietnamese, her guidebook identifies her as Japanese. Yet language is not an exclusive marker of national identity either, for she later meets James, a Japanese-speaking Caucasian who claims to be Japanese. When Kazuko asks him how this happened, he throws her question back at her: "What about you? How did you become Japanese?" Tellingly, both questions are left unanswered. If identity is this arbitrary, it is merely an illusion. And so is the idea that each person has a single self in the first place.

The story "Saint George and the Translator" was originally called "The Wound in the Alphabet," (*Arufabetto no kizuguchi*), which in turn is a translation of "Der Wunde Punkt im Alphabet," the story by the German writer Anne Duden that the narrator of Tawada's story is translating. To avoid confusion with Duden's story, Tawada later changed the title to "Transplanting Letters" (*Moji-ishoku*). Nevertheless, the original title has interesting implications for Tawada's text.

Take, for instance, the "O's" that cover the page the narrator is translating in the opening scene. Seemingly backed by a white wall she can't break through, they frustrate her until she blackens all of them in. By filling in the "O's," the narrator has turned the white wall into a kind of tunnel, an entrance into the foreign language that allows her to pass each word over to the other side—in other words, to translate (*übersetzen*, the German word for translation, contains the meaning "to pass something over to the other side"). But then again, these blackened "O's" might also be "wounds in the alphabet" that the narrator scratches out with the tip of her fountain pen. The Japanese verb *kaku* ("to write") is homonymous with another verb that means "to scratch," suggesting an etymological connection between the two. The Chinese character for "creation" can also mean "wound." When Duden's *wunde* is translated into Japanese, it takes on an extra layer of meaning—to wound is also to create. And if writing itself began as an act of scratching figures, "creating wounds," then translation is the process of inscribing those wounds into a foreign language.

In "The Task of the Translator," Walter Benjamin emphasizes the importance of "a literal rendering of the syntax which proves words rather than sentences to be the primary element of the translator." The narrator of "Saint George and the Translator" follows his advice, sticking as closely as possible to the German syntax, breaking Duden's sentences into fragments, savoring the foreignness of each word as she carefully passes it over to the other side. While perhaps not the "pure language" Benjamin was aiming for, the jumble of words and phrases of her translation definitely have a poetic power that can best be appreciated when the text is read aloud.

A fragmented style is perhaps most appropriate for translating the dragon, a creature composed of fragments from a wide variety of animal species. Dragons are also occasionally hermaphrodites, which poses a particular problem for the translator—which pronoun should she use? She finally decides to stick with "he," which in Japanese is *kare*, a word that originally referred to things as well as people, and, until the early twentieth century, was a pronoun used for both men and women. The Chinese character for *kare* is also contained in words like *kanata*, which refers to a loosely defined, faraway place ("over there") and *higan*, which literally means "the other side": The dragon, who insists on violating all human taboos, is totally alien—a creature, we might say, from "the other side."

Like much of the Japanese language in use today, the word *kare* was created through translation after Japan was opened to the West in the nineteenth century. When intellectuals discovered that there were no equivalents in Japanese for Western pronouns or abstract concepts such as freedom, individuality, society, art, rights (as in human rights) or beauty (in the abstract sense), it appeared to them that the Japanese language was full of holes, which they immediately set about plugging up. They did this by inventing new words, or by assigning new meanings to old ones. In many cases, however, the new words didn't fit precisely into the holes they were meant to fill, and a sense of incompatibility still lingers around these words. Now that their origin in translation has all but been forgotten, however, the words are, in a sense, dead. By connecting the pronoun *kare* to its older usage in words like *kanata* and *higan*, Tawada has not only made it more suitable for referring to the alien nature of the dragon. She has also dug *kare* out of its hole, creating another "wound in the alphabet," and in the process, bringing the word back to life. It seems a shame to have to translate it back to "he."

The protagonist's translation that is imbedded in her own narration is composed of long flowing sentences without a single comma (in my translation I use commas only in the sections of dialogue). This style seems particularly well suited to Ei, the narrator's translator-turned-novelist friend ("Ei" is pronounced like the letter "A" rather than the German word for "egg"), who advises the narrator to translate whole sentences in a single breath. Ei's condescending attitude toward translation is, I fear, shared by many in the U.S., despite the recent boom in translation studies. If we can think of Ei as representing the demands of the market, and the narrator as the opposite extreme, aiming for Benjamin's dream of a "pure language," most literary translators are caught somewhere in between.

Which brings me to my final point—the relationship between the narrator and "the author." While the narrator is attracted to the author, the author seems to have little need for the narrator, and finally leaves her behind. This, it seems to me, is a fairly accurate depiction of the author-translator relationship. Translators need authors more than authors need translators. Yet Tawada's position as a writer, intentionally placing herself on the border (or, as she herself puts it, "in the ravine") between German and Japanese, is somewhat akin to the translator, who is always caught between two languages.

At one point the nameless narrator looks at the author's face and sees only an "O." If this "O" is like one of the tunnels the narrator scratches out with her fountain pen, then the translator, while appearing subservient, is actually using the author as a means to enter a foreign language. And enter it she does, for with the appearance of multiple Saint Georges, the boundary between her life on the island and the work she has been translating collapses, and she finds herself trapped in the story, unable to go anywhere except into the sea. This open-ended conclusion lends an entirely new meaning to that old saw "lost in translation." But then again, inside a text is probably where translators (and writers as well) really belong. I myself hope to stay "lost in translation" for some time to come.